GAMBLING PROSTITUTION AND DRUGS

BY Frederick Lee Toomer

FREDERICK LEE TOOMER

COPYRIGHT

GAMBLING PROSTITUTION AND DRUGS
Presented by F. READY PUBLISHING
Copyright 2020 Fredrick Toomer
ALL RIGHTS RESERVED
F.READYPUBLISHING@GMAIL.COM

TABLE OF CONTENTS

ACKNOWLEDGMENTS

This book is dedicated to my fourth-grade teacher, Ms. Bullock, who helped change my life. She was the one who gave me the inspiration that turned into a lifelong dream to write a book.

Years ago, what was I going to write about? Not until I lived this element called life. I decided at one point I wanted to prefill one of my lifelong dreams in life.

My inspiration came from an extensive list of writers. These are Donald Goines, Robert Beck, better known as Iceberg slim, Dennis Kimble, and many more. I would like to thank all the people who inspired every word in this book.

I would like to thank the whole team who helped put this book together. I would like to thank my cover designer, Vinit29 from Fiverr.com and all editing done by F. READYPUBLISHING

Finally, I would like to thank my social media promoter, Vibe with Fredd at Instagram.com.

Please follow GAMBLING PROSTITUTION AND DRUGS ON THE FOLLOWING HANDLES:

INTRODUCTION

Welcome to **GAMBLING PROSTITUTION AND DRUGS**.

Before producing this book, I asked myself, how do I start this story about my life? Now... you probably would be asking what inspired me to write this book? Honestly, I got to a very lonely point in my journey where I wanted to put all my life experiences on paper. It seemed like this is the only way I can cleanse myself and deal with the harsh realities that played in my life.

My name is Fredrick Lee Toomer, born December 14, 1975, at 11:18pm on a very chilly winter Sunday in Queen's General Hospital, as I would hear my mom tell it. I'm the son of Jerome and Denise Toomer. I'm the oldest of two sisters and one brother.

We grew up in South Jamaica Queens, on a street called Liverpool, in a small two-bedroom third-floor apartment.

As I write this book, it makes me dig very deep into my past and think about the people who passed through my life. Some of the memories makes me laugh, and some make me cry. I'll tell you this, though each person and each experience that came my way, had some type of impact on my life. My time growing up in New York City was one long exciting spontaneous journey.

As you read this book, I hope you can identify with my story as I unveil myself, and in the process, learn different things about myself and gain some clarity of the harsh realities that I lived through out this book. I hope my story touches your minds and enriches your souls.

In this book, I will talk about growing up in one of the most crime-infested areas on the south side of Queens in New York City. I will tell the story of my rough experiences and how crack destroyed Black families all around the country including mine.

Finally, I will discuss my dreams of becoming an "entrepreneur."

Let us go on!

I started out as a Manhattan messenger, then a door-to-door salesperson. Looking "desperately" to find the enterprising spirit, I swung into a life of crime and started out as a pimp on the legendary New York City streets, then rising the ranks in the world of prostitution.

In this book, you will learn how a place called Atlantic City changed I and my family's lives forever and how it made me desperately hunt for the entrepreneurial spirit by any means necessary.

My mind ran through many moments, full of questions, seeking answers, imaginations crept in, I had always wanted to discover myself.

Weighing my background, I asked myself one day, "when my father started his business from a Shoestring, did he have the ambitious spirit?" Or "did my grandfather have it when he started

C.T. exterminating in 1975, the same year I was born?" This entrepreneurial spirit is inherited from generations to generations. Greed, ambition, dreamers, are these the true ingredients needed for entrepreneurial success?

They say one out of every ten businesses make it. If this is true, in which it is, then I love the book, the POWER OF BROKE by Daymond John. He talks about people who overcame great obstacles to rise to financial freedom.

My fight for financial freedom hasn't been an easy journey. In my long hunt for success, I decided I would write this book and maybe the readers can learn from my experiences.

This is not a book about the success story of a great guy, who made millions of dollars out of the blues. Of course, we all have our different stories to tell. Specifically, this is a story of a young entrepreneur, who grew up on the south side of Queens, New York. It's a story of a regular guy with ambitions for financial freedom.

In gaining this freedom, I decided to take some unconventional risks. The reality is, we always hear about celebrities and the stories of how they made it thus far. I decided to write GAMBLING PROSTITUTION AND DRUGS, so I can tell my story, as an average individual.

In life, does it matter how much money we have? Or are we just all controlled by money? The reality is, anybody can become wealthy with hard work and dedication in a plan quoted in the book, the BLACK TITAN, the A.G. GASTON STORY. His book is a must-read on how to become wealthy.

Years later when I found riches, I did not understand the money game that the wealthy has mastered, so I would always end up penniless from time to time. I hope my readers and young people who inspire to become financially free can learn from my mistakes.

Through my journey in life, I have seen businesses built from the ground floor. I know what it is to believe in something and risk everything you must make it work and you still come up short. That is what happened to my partner and I when we started www.bestkeptsecrets69.com in 2004. We risked everything we had, we took a shot, and it just did not work and years later I understood why. I have experienced the upside and the downside of business.

My mentor had a luxurious living room he like to call the situation room where we drink cognac and sniff cocaine. Whenever we would sit there, he used to tell me, "Fred, the faster you get over it, the quicker you can do it again!" He told me this after I lost everything and had to start from nothing. This advice came from a man that made millions in prostitution and real estate. At one point, he lost it all and had to rebuild.

One of life's most valuable lessons is learning from your experiences, getting to know yourself, your weaknesses and your strengths and admitting to yourself where you are weak.

Life is our best teacher. Whether you want to learn or not, it is totally up to the individual.

In business, nothing comes easy that's worth having. We must take advantage of every brake that comes our way. We must learn from our mistakes, decide to stay true to ourselves, be mentally strong and never give into weak emotions.

The most essential element than anything else is "learning self-value." It does not matter how much money you have. If you do not have any self-value, you will find yourself on top of a building ready to jump.

Like a lot of people who decided after losing all their money, because they never had true self-worth, they didn't only lose their money, they lost themselves too.

True knowledge of self is worth more than any amount of money you could make in your lifetime. Being able to deal with everyone, either rich or poor, is the "true wealth." What is true wealth? Well, in my opinion, let me say it this way.

You see many lottery winners, sports athletes and entertainers go bankrupt and end up always having nothing all the time. They never really understood the true essence of wealth. Being able to understand the "science behind wealth" is the "key."

Dennis Kimble, the author of WEALTH CHOICE quoted in his book that "as Black men, we are not free until we are financially free." His book is a must read. As people, we should always learn the rules to the money game.

People do all types of evil things for money. They say money brings out what type of person you really are, and it is true. Look at how people will change over a lot of money or not enough money.

I learned in life, nothing is more important than having a peace of mind and being able to help the people around you grow. That is the true wealth, the improvement of humanity.

This book is a true story! As you read this book, know that everything you will read is true. I have lived all my life experiences, good or bad.

Therefore, getting to this point to be able to write this book about my life is a true blessing from the creator above. I give praises and thanks to the creator for making this book a reality.

Without further due, F. READY Publishing presents **"GAMBLING PROSTITUTION AND DRUGS."**

CHAPTER 1

A 70s BABY AND 80s KID

As far back as I can remember some of my most memorable times as a kid, it brings tears to my eyes thinking about how much has changed. My father worked at C.T Exterminating. This was his father's business that started in 1975.

The Mets played baseball in Flushing, where a lot of their customers were located. My father was a die-hard Mets fan, and I would never think thirty years later that Flushing, New York would be the birthplace of F. READY PUBLISHING.

As a kid, we did not live that far from shea stadium. While driving, my father would ask me, you want to go to the ball game? I would say yes. Immediately, he would turn right off the Van Wyck expressway and to Shea Stadium we would go!

At that time, I was five years old. The Mets were not a big contender in those days, so it was easy to get in the stadium. Those childhood memories with my dad would stay with me a lifetime.

Watching my father get up early and go to work, he showed me what a man was about. I didn't need a role model. I had my pops and I thought he was the greatest father there was. Years later, our relationship would take a turn for the worse.

I was born on December 14, 1975, in Queens General hospital in New York city at 11:18pm, and on a chilly winter Sunday, I would join this world. In 1975, our country's President was Gerald Ford. The Mayor of New York City was Abraham Beam.

It was the seventies disco era. The top song in the country was KC and the sunshine ban singing that's the way I like it.

Our country's unemployment rate was at 8.2% and the Vietnam war ended in 1975 after a long controversial ten years.

On April 4, 1975, in Albuquerque, New Mexico, Microsoft is born, founded by Bill Gates and Paul Allen.

It was the start of the computer revolution.

By then, the richest person in the world was J. Paul Getty and the most powerful company was Exxon.

I was born to a beautiful mother, very cunning, very convincing, very funny and a great personality that can attract anybody. Knowing my mother, she would have been great at sales. I think in some ways she never lived up to her full potential.

My father didn't want anything to do with me as a kid. He tried to say I didn't belong to him. My mother use to tell me this all the time as I got older.

Even to this day, I never confronted my father about it.

My mother was sixteen and my father was eighteen. I was two years old when they were married in July 1977. I do not think they were ever supposed to be together. I had never seen them happy as a couple and could remember them arguing all the time.

My mother would never let me forget how she struggled with me when I was a baby, not having my father in our life. I guess you can say their marriage was cursed from the beginning.

On their wedding day, my uncles, Bishop, and Marvin were both Vietnam vets. They would get into a heated family dispute! Marvin ended up accidentally strangling Bishop on my grandmother's steps! This was talked about for years on my mother's side of the family.

In later years, I would hear Marvin say he would see Bishop come out the subway and I would get a spooky feeling when I would hear Marvin reveal that deep dark secret. It was rumored that my grandmother would make sure Marvin never went to jail.

What happened exactly? Nobody knew!

It would leave a black cloud over my family forever.

As a kid growing up, I would see my mother and father get into some very nasty arguments. I can remember as a kid walking into the kitchen and witnessing my mother holding a knife to my father for not letting her leave.

I could remember I just sadly stood and watched with fear and confusion! As far back as I can remember, my household had its good times and troubled times.

I went to school in Forest Hills. I was placed in a special ed program in public school 101. Prior to that, I attended a Catholic school. School to me at times was very confusing. I loved to read about history, but I hated mathematics. I was not incredibly talented at sports; I was a short, small kid.

I remember when I went to public school 160, there were boys my age that bullied me all the time. Then years later, I would become the bully.

Growing up in South Jamaica, "you had to be tuff." If you were soft, you would become an easy prey for kids to harass you around the neighborhood.

I remember as a kid, my mother would send me to the store. There were some neighborhood kids that use to hangout. One of them use to pick on me all the time and I did not understand why. I was a peaceful kid; I did not have any violence in my heart.

Growing up in the slums can change a kid, I remember this same kid punching me in the face and I did nothing. There was a bigger kid there saying you should have fought. Those words, and that punch the kid hit me with, mixed with that embarrassing moment of fear would stay with me forever.

When that happened to me, one thing came into in my mind… I must get tuff to survive in this ghetto!

As far back as I can remember, one of my most horrifying childhood memories is when my left eye popped out my head!

Well, it happened like this… I was in my room playing too much. I guess, overly being a kid. My mother did give me a fierce warning before it happened. Do you think I listened to her? Of course not! As she was whipping my ass, the belt buckle slipped and popped my left eye out.

My father had to come in early from work and he screamed at me. On his way driving to Queen's General hospital, this was the same hospital I was born in. My oldest Aunt Karen would be the only person that showed up I would never forget her for that.

I could remember being hooked up to all those tubes, laying on the bed helpless. It was an extremely scary experience for me and for everyone around.

They told me I had 20/80 vision and was permanently almost blind in my left eye. And here is my mother, asking me to tell the hospital it happened outside while playing with other kids. And one of the kids threw a stick at me and my eye popped out.

Well, this is my mother, my precious mother. I could not but do what she asked. My mother did not want them to take me for child abuse.

After that incident, I was almost blind in one eye. I can honestly say I did not feel the same way about her. I guess, sometimes you must take the hand your dealt, and play it out.

This is how my life would start!

The 80's came to be one of our most memorable decades. By 1982, I was seven years old, Ronald Reagan was President of the United States and Ed Koch was the Mayor of New York City.

Our country's unemployment rate was at 10.8% and the Richest person in the world was Saudi businessperson, Adnan Khashoggi. Our most powerful company was Exxon.

I was busted out the neighborhood and sent to public school 101 in Forest Hills where I was placed in a special ed program. I do not know all the details; it was told to me. I was assessed and evaluated with a learning disability.

All I know is, when school started again in September, a yellow bus was waiting outside, taking me to public school 101 every day.

Prior to public school 101, I attended two Catholic schools and a public school. I was left back twice in the first grade, so I was eight years old in the second grade. I was not doing any good in the schools they placed me in.

Waking up every day and attending public school 101 elementary school in Forest Hills was a unique experience than going to school in my ghetto in South Jamaica Queens. Forest Hills was the wealthy part of Queens. It gave me a totally different outlook on life.

I genuinely loved the experience of leaving my tuff neighborhood and exploring various parts of Queens. Up until that point, school seemed confusing, and a waste of time and I had a tough time concentrating.

I really did not take school seriously until public school 101. The classes were much smaller than the other schools and the teachers were very friendly. I was able to have a good relationship with almost all of them.

While I was trying to get used to my new school, South Jamaica was falling victim to one of the biggest drug epidemics this country has ever seen. The 1980s brought a new crime wave to South Jamaica Queen's drug kingpins like Lorenzo Nichols, better known as Fat Cat, Kenneth McGriff, who was known as Supreme, the head of the Supreme team and Laurelton's own Thomas Mickens, better known as Tony Montana.

These notorious Southside hustlers would all carve out their piece of Queens. A thing called crack would hit the scenes and turn the whole South Jamaica to fiends. In 1966, despite the community efforts, South Jamaica was designated a poverty zone. All these social problems would fuel the cocaine crack epidemic.

Black ghettos all around the world would feel the worse of it. Mothers abandoning their children, fathers falling deeper into poverty and

BLACK ON BLACK crime would rise to an all-time high. The crack era would have a profound effect on generations to come to a point they would be known as crack babies.

Crack would make its way into suburban neighborhoods and that's when you started seeing Nancy Regan on tv in commercials saying, "just say no". Just tell me, where was she when this drug was destroying Black ghettos all around the country? It only started becoming an epidemic when it started affecting beautiful white communities across the country.

It was very similar to the heroin epidemic of the sixties. South Jamaica's crime wave would even be exploited by other crime entities. The Gambino crime family headed by a notorious gangster known as the Teflon Don on the streets, better known as John Gotti, would claim a piece of South Jamaica as well.

I could remember when my father was driving, and we were riding down the Vanwyck expressway. The only tow trucks you would see towing any cars would be Jamaica towing. The Gambino crime family on liberty avenue in South Jamaica made its impact. All the junk yards and everything was rumored to be controlled by John Gotti.

By April 4, 1992, the Gambino family were indicted by the testimony of fellow Gambino top associate, Sammy the bull Gravano which indicted John Gotti in another family associate would be found guilty of all charges. They were sentenced to life in prison without parole.

By December 14, 1992, by my sixteenth birthday, the legendary gangster would turn himself in. It was the end of an era for organized crime. The 1980s Black communities all around the country would feel this crack boom. Years later America would learn the real reason for this drug epidemic. Do you remember the Iran contra hearings with Oliver North? The whole epidemic was fueled by the Ronald Reagan administration to help fund the Vietcong.

At seven years old, I already knew what I wanted to be when I grew up. I wanted to be my own boss, just like my father, he was his own boss. I love the 1980s hit tv show "Dallas", I love watching the character JR Ewing played with all his cutthroat business tactics.

The 80s would shape up to be one of our most memorable decades from your Iran contra hearings, to crack destroying families across America, to your Rubik's cube becoming one of your most popular hand games ever, to the Atari 2600 being the first video game created, to Michael Jackson selling 66 million copies of the thriller album, and to your legendary E.T movie being one of your most top-grossing movies of the decade.

I will always remember the 1980s!

CHAPTER 2
Ms. BULLOCKS CLASS

Well, it was 1986. I was in the fourth grade and Ms. Bullock was my fourth-grade teacher and two unforgettable things would happen that year.

The Mets would beat the Boston Red Sox in a historical seven-game series. In school, two people became a part of my young journey and had an extreme impact on my childhood and my life—Ms. Bullock and my guidance counselor, Mr. Ross. By this time, I was already getting used to my daily bus trips to school.

While riding the school bus, I would meet a childhood best friend I would hang with for the next eight years. His name was Sharper Anderson.

When I first met Sharper, he thought he was the tougher kid until he noticed me beat up a kid much bigger than I was. After that, we had no problems anymore. Ms. Bullock was my fourth-grade teacher. She was a middle-aged Black woman with a beautiful gospel voice. She was kind and taught me to enjoy reading and not to be afraid to learn.

Ms. Bullock was like my mother while I was

in her classroom. I could never describe in words what she meant to me and how she helped me change my life to this day. I was a very disturbed kid and very disruptive in class. Ms. Bullock made me respect her and taught me it was okay to learn. As I talk about her, it brings tears to my eyes.

Ms. Bullock's class was the class that helped me grow and helped me look at life differently. While attending her class, I would fall in love with Black history. Sadly, years later after I dropped out of high school, I was eighteen years old and haven't seen her in years.

I had gotten a job with a wholesale company. I was selling products, business to business calculators and small toys for kids. These were products that would cost no more than ten dollars.

I was on Hillside Avenue in Queens when I walked into a beauty salon. I saw Ms. Bullock sitting there with a beautiful head of grey. She had aged a great deal. She glanced at me as if she remembered who I was. I felt so ashamed that she saw me doing this. I should have been finishing high school or starting college. I felt like I owed her an excuse. I left immediately with embarrassment hoping in my mind she didn't remember me.

However, I knew she knew who I was. Those moments of embarrassment would haunt me for the rest of my life. She was the one teacher I respected and learned a lot from. Down the hall in her classroom, I would meet a man. His name was Mr. Ross and would be my guidance counselor until I was sixteen years old.

When I first met this man as a young child, I can remember he was a big Jewish man with a very gentle demeanor. I really didn't understand what his purpose was for me. Was he there to help me with my learning disability? I didn't trust him very much.

This strange man the school put in my life would take some time to get used to. He always asked me questions about the school. I remember he was extremely easy to talk to. Eventually, he made me feel comfortable around him.

In Ms. Bullock's class, I just didn't learn how to read, and I just didn't meet my new guidance counselor. I also learned how to respect a classroom.

One day when I was acting out in her class, Ms. Bullock took time out her afternoon to take me home to my father. Getting home, I told him what I did, and Ms. Bullock told my father not to beat me. Yeah, I still got a whipping that evening!

Ms. Bullock's class was the class that helped me grow up and look at life in school differently. Learning and reading about Martin Luther King, Marcus Garvey, and Harriet Tubman just to name a few. Reading about these people put me in touch with my Black heritage. She taught me to appreciate reading whenever I went to visit the school after attending Russell sage. All the teachers from all my classes always told me, "Make sure you visit Ms. Bullock's class" and I always did.

I was promoted to the fifth grade that year. I deeply missed her after that year. I miss her now.

Thank you, Ms. Bullock.

CHAPTER 3
WELCOME TO ALANTIC CITY

Resort International would be the first casino on the historical boardwalk. Gambling was passed in 1976, in all efforts to restore Atlantic City.

As I sit here and write this book it makes me think about the first time, I arrived in Atlantic Cities golden age era. I was eight years old, and it was the summer of 1983. I remember my father driving all of us in his baby blue Pontiac Catalina. It was I and my two sisters in the back and my mother on the passenger side. I can remember my father driving up to the Playboy's fancy casino parking valet located by the entrance of the boardwalk. It was an exciting memory.

As we would drive up, the valet boys would rush to the car, open the door, and greet the whole family with class. I felt like the richest kid in the world. I would never forget that feeling of being rich or those beautiful sexy playboy bunnies walking around the casino lobby. The Playboy casino owned by legendary adult magazine owner Hugh Hefner, would open on April 14, 1981.

The casino would have a short stay in Atlantic

City by 1984. It would be renamed "The Atlantis." As I write about Atlantic City, I can tell you I had some of the greatest times of my life and some of the worst times in this place called paradise.

When you come to any of these towns where gambling is the town's survival, they don't tell you the horrors of the casino industry. A casino's job is to paint a picture of easy money and relaxation. Casinos are the biggest pimps in the world because everyone likes to buy a dream.

In this industry, they will never tell you the longer they can get you to stay, all your dreams can be over. It can happen within a second, with just a spin of the slot machine or a roll of the dice. You could be hooked for life because the mental side of gambling is way worse than just losing your money. In all reality, is gambling just a get rich dream?

The cold-blooded reality of it is, I don't care what casino you walk into. There are two things they never run out of and that is time and money. Remember there are no clocks or windows in casinos. They want you not only to lose your money. However, they want you to lose track of reality and build a false fantasy so they can control your destiny.

The Cardinal rule in casinos is this… the longer they can get you to stay, the more money you will play. Many times, I ask myself, do most people have the time and money to beat them? Did my parents? In every casino, there are no chains or locks on the doors. You can always leave or come in any time you want to.

However, it's the mental lock that keeps us there. The feeling of winning money!

I have been around gambling all my life. I remember as a kid my mother would take me to Aqueduct Racetrack. I would watch people holla and go crazy for their horse to win and if it didn't close your ears. I witnessed at once as a child what gambling can do to an individual. By 1986 gambling destroyed my family and destroyed my father's business. I remember the horrors of gambling and how it affected my family.

When my mother and father would get rooms in these casinos, they would leave myself and my sisters in the room all night. At least that was okay because when they went completely broke, there would be times we couldn't get a room. We would sleep in the car from night to night. We would sometimes have no money or food to eat, it seemed like a big adventure.

There were times when my father would call up some of his customers he knew and borrow money. This was extremely embarrassing for him.

The worse thing with gambling is, when you win, it's like a junkie getting high, you want to chase that feeling. The same thing with a gambler. They want to chase that feeling of winning. I could remember my mother one time running in the room full of excitement, screaming that she had just won five thousand dollars! That was the worst thing that could have happened to her. She was hooked for life.

Atlantic City was tuff on my family. My sisters and I would miss a lot of school. When I did go, I did not know what was going on. There were times when my mother would say anything to my father to get there. I hated my life as a kid sleeping in the car. Even more, I hated my father for not being sterner, and letting his family go through this.

As a kid, I ran away several times and my parents could not understand why. My father would complain about how dreadful things were and how he was heavily in debt to loan sharks. Was his dream of becoming a successful business owner in jeopardy? They say behind every successful man, there is a successful woman. Is this true in all cases? Was it him or did he have the right woman on his side with the right mindset? Did my mother fall victim to get rich dreams and schemes of gambling? What would she say or do to my father for him to constantly put his business and family at risk?

All these questions circled my mind on why my family struggled so badly. It was sad to see my father go to work just to lose everything in Atlantic City.

My mother complained about my father not having any medical insurance because my grandfather wouldn't put him on the books. She had supposedly found a doctor that she could go to out there and could treat her for any medical conditions.

One thing about my mother you never knew. When she was telling the truth, she had so many different stories.

I could remember one time we we're staying at the Taffy motel, it's still there to this day located in Absecon on the White horse pike. My mother stormed in the room yelling that two men had beaten her. My father almost went crazy! They put all of us in the car and my father got his pipe out and went looking for them.

As we drove to a strange neighborhood near Atlantic City, my sisters and I sat in the back confused and scared, watching my father drive with anger. The reality is, we never found anyone. Was it another story? Who knows what really happened that night?

With all these things going on, one early morning, coming back from Atlantic City, my mother almost had my brother Robby on the Garden State parkway. She started having labor pains. We had to stop the car and the police came and took her to the hospital. She would arrive later that day with a new member of the family; my younger brother "Robert Toomer," who would be my mother and father last and their favorite.

Robby would be born on June 6, 1987. I thought to have a younger baby brother was the best feeling in the world. As much as I adored Robert, years later, our relationship would turn into pure confusion.

Crazy thing was, when he was born, I was happy to have a brother. Even with Robert being born, I always wished I had a brother my age. I wished Roxanne my younger sister was my younger brother. My family's life was in shambles.

I was eleven in the fourth grade, and I didn't understand life or where it was going. When my brother Robert arrived, we started to become a real family again. At times it seems like I was just flowing along with time.

The best times I had was coming home from school and playing stickball with my friends. I loved baseball as a kid. I wanted something to take me away from my home because I was tired of living in the same small room with my sisters. I was starting to get older and realizing how important money was.

At that time, the criminal life started to influence my mind. It was one thing to be black and proud. However, how could you really be proud of being black if you're broke all the time? And all you see around you is crime in a struggle, and the wrong is the right. Those crack dealers that use to stand on the corner with their Kangol hats twisted to the side and those big goose coats. Adidas sneakers in big gold rope chains with wads of money.

As a young man witnessing all of this, it was exceedingly difficult for it not to be an influence on my mind, especially when you don't have a dime. I had nothing as a young kid attending school.

Sometimes, I had holes in my sneakers and my pants. In the ghetto, it's all about looking rich and you adapt to what you see around you.

It seems like the condition I watched my father struggle was playing out in my life too. Do I have any hope? Was getting a good education a key out of the ghetto? Atlantic City was the start of our problems. Before Atlantic City, we had a normal family life.

I finished the fifth and sixth grades and graduated from public school 101 elementary school.

Russell Sage Junior High School would become my next journey.

CHAPTER 4
THE 90s: A TEENAGE LOVE

The year was 1990 and I was now fourteen years old. I had graduated from public school 101. It was time to be a big boy and step out into the world. No more yellow school bus, no more door-to-door pick-up anymore.

My parents, a week prior to me starting at Russell Sage showed me how to get there on the bus. Every morning, I would leave and walk to my best friend's Sharper house, and we would walk to Sutphin Blvd and catch the E train to school. It was a new experience in life, I felt like I was gaining independence.

And now, I could really see what New York city was like. By age fourteen I had got bigger. I was a short stocky kid with a football player build.

On the bus in school, I had already beaten up a couple of kids who tried to bully me. It made me think back to when I was that small timid kid in public school 160 elementary school. I used to get beat up all the time.

There was one kid I had to fight every day. It was so bad my father had to teach me and force me to fight. I was a peaceful kid. However, in the ghetto where young Black kids grow up, it was killed or be killed.

I was not that small timid kid anymore. I was no longer getting bullied. Those times passed quickly and now I became the bully.

That year, I started the seventh grade in special ed in Russell Sage junior high school located in Forest Hills Queens. Russell Sage was different from the schools in my neighborhood. It was kids from all cultures that attended. My new school in some ways forced me to grow up and it motivated me to learn!

Although deep down, I was a very shy kid. This experience would help me open myself.

I think back and I remember my first day. I was extremely nervous and curious. My special ed class was located on the third floor.

Our classes were separated from the regular ed classes and had under twelve kids. When you are evaluated with a learning disability, it is considered that you learn or comprehend at a slower pace, so they place you in smaller classes.

I felt comfortable to be in a new environment. There were girls from all diverse cultures. Some of them were pretty. Up until that point I've had crushes on girls but never no real girlfriend. I was more into going home and playing sports with my friends.

The teachers were cool. I had a good relationship with most of them. I would run into

Mr. Ross, my old public school guidance counselor who I met in Ms. Bullock's fourth-grade class. We would meet every Monday down the hall from my homeroom. Mr. Ross told me my reading was on grade level and I would have one mainstream class which would be English.

At first, when I attended the class, I thought all the kids were so much smarter than me. It was quite different from my special ed class. These were full regular ed classes. Deep down inside, I loved the challenge of learning with these kids on their level. I guess I was not so slow after all. My new mainstream class was tuff.

Soon, I would get used to it. The seventh grade in Russell Sage was an exciting new beginning and exciting new school! I made sure I did not miss any days. My friend Sharper and I went to the same school, just different classes. We would always meet up every day after school and take the train home together.

Going to school was an escape from my tuff neighborhood and dysfunctional family. By that time, my father was very deeply in debt with loan sharks. I would hear a lot of arguing about money between my mother and father.

My father seemed very frustrated all the time. He paid me to work with him on weekends. With the money he paid me, I would buy my school clothes.

My father was in a tuff predicament. He started FM Pest Control in 1981 from a Shoestring. I remember many times while lying on the couch in our living room—which he had turned into a small office—I would hear him on the phone calling up his father's customers. He was trying to see who wanted to come with him to his new business. It was a gutsy move by my Pops.

However, he was ready to be his own boss. I wanted to be part of what he was trying to build. I desperately wanted him to get out of debt. My mother had great personal service skills. She had a pretty voice over the phone which the male customers loved. I learned at a young age the difference between having good and bad money management skills. Handling money poorly when you are in business will put a burden on the survival of the business.

My father taught me that being on time, being courteous and being a good conversationalist was extremely important. I made sure I watched everything my father did and how he dealt with his customers. The elements that I learned in running and starting a small business by watching my mother and father was priceless information. I couldn't learn that in a classroom.

My father on the weekends use to get me up at six am in the morning. We would be at our first customer's house at seven am and by one pm, we would have done at least twenty jobs. His work ethic was hardcore. Those weekends with my father were everything to me and this would give me a lifetime of wisdom.

It was cool working all over the five boroughs. I learned a lot on how to get around New York city. I learned at an early age that you cannot become wealthy working for anyone else.

For you to become wealthy, you must be the one that's in control. Atlantic City and the debt that my father acquired stopped my mother and father from becoming successful Black business owners.

As a young kid, I and my sisters played a lot. I remember we made a game up called business. It was silly but fun. For the object of the game, we had to get the leftover coupons from the Sunday papers. Whoever had the most coupons would win. The coupons represented play money when we were young. We were a real family. When we struggled, we struggled as a family.

My two sisters attended public school fifty located on liberty avenue, about a ten-minute walk from the house. They were both very smart and beautiful girls. As my year in seventh grade went past, three things started happening to me. I was starting to get older, my needs for female companionship started to grow and my want for money started to be evident.

Around the neighborhood, there were several drug dealers that tried to recruit me. My father was extremely strict, he would have killed me. However, it still did not stop those thoughts from going through my mind. Would my father's demanding work ethics win me over or the flash of the streets? I used to ask myself all the time, how do you fight off this poverty disease?

Over the next year, I would finish the seventh grade in Russell Sage. Russell Sage was a new beginning, but it was also time to look to the future.

The nineties were the start of a new decade. Our President of the United States was George H. W. Bush. Our Mayor of New York City was the first Black American to get into Gracie mansion, David Dinkins who would serve two terms as Mayor.

After the recession filled eighties, our nation's unemployment rate in the nineties would drop to 5.6%. The decade before our unemployment rate was at 10.8%. Bill Gates was now the richest man in the world worth over twelve billion dollars. In our most powerful company was General Motors. The nineties was the start of an economic boom. It was the start of the tech age companies like Amazon, created by Jeff Bezos on July 5, 1994, in Seattle Washington.

Netflix would be created on August 29, 1997, in Scott Valley California by Reed Hastings and Marc Randolph. Google, another giant would be born September 4, 1998, in Menlo California by Larry Page and Sergey Brin. Yahoo would be born March 2, 1995, by Jerry Yang and David filo just to name a few. These companies and many more would change the world and become a part of our daily life in years to come.

In 1991, our country would enter the gulf war which in years to come the US military would spend a long time in the Middle east. In 1992, I was sixteen years old, and I was in my last year of Russell Sage. By this time, Sharper and I were in the same class. We were some of the most feared seniors that walked around Russell Sage. No one bothered us.

It was about twenty of us that were bussed in from South Jamaica every day to this beautiful suburban neighborhood. In Forest Hills Queens, these kids, mostly all of them were from South Jamaica. And were sent there just like me.

We all attended Russell Sage special ed program. A lot of these kids had unbelievably unruly behavior problems. On the third floor where all the special ed programs were located, there were always plenty of disturbances. Kids would get into fights all the time.

They brought in Mr. Segal from I-S eight located on the south side of Queens New York. I-S eight was rated one of the worse junior high schools in Queens and that is where all the kids from the neighborhood went. Mr. Segal was more experienced in dealing with these kids. I created a real complex for myself as a real bully.

There were several times I ended up in his office in school. I was feared and was feared around the neighborhood. They called me big Fred. I guess that name stuck because of my stocky size. I felt like the heavyweight champion at the time, Mike Tyson. I was built like him and had a strong right just like him.

The street dealers around the neighborhood started to respect and try to recruit me. I can remember everything started to change for me at Russell Sage.

I remember meeting my first girlfriend, her name was Mia Gibbs. She was a teenage love. Mia was the first in everything. She was the first real love I experienced and shared my innocents with and broke my heart.

Mia at the time was fifteen going on thirty with an intellectual type of look. I met Mia passing her on the third floor where all the special ed classes were located. Down the hall from the regular ed classrooms, she was on her way to her next class. Mia was the most beautiful girl in my eyes. She had these beautiful dimples when she smiled, she could light up a room, she was genuinely nice and pleasant to talk to.

I fell in love with Mia's smile instantly. She was dressed very professionally like a secretary who worked in an office. Mia never struck me as a regular schoolgirl.

I can remember when I first saw her, I was very shy, but the words made it out my mouth. I said to her you look very nice today. She smiled with those beautiful dimples, and she said thank you. From that point on, any time I saw her, we would stop for a moment and talk to each other.

Mia Gibbs was from Regal Park in Queens. She lived with her mother and two older brothers. Mia and I would become remarkably close in no time and would start passing love letters to each other. We would enjoy long walks after school and just enjoy our time together. I think back to when we both gave our innocents to each other; we were young and in love.

We talked about being intimate for weeks until one day we went to my house in South Jamaica.

That day, my parents were in Atlantic City and my two sisters were in their room. Mia and I snuck into my parent's room.

We sat on the bed and for some brief nervous moments, we just looked in each other's eyes, then we started kissing very romantically. We both held each other closely as I removed her panties.

I said to myself, wow, I couldn't believe it for the first time I saw a girl's vagina! My penis would get fully erect as she lets me gently inside her for the first time.

It felt so good to experience being with a female. I became scared of getting her pregnant and immediately pulled out of her.

I was okay with my first sexual experience with her however, I knew the best was yet to come.

After that time, I and Mia would pleasure each other all the time; most mornings before school at her apartment in Regal Park. After a while, we would pleasure each other everywhere. At Coney Island in Nathan's bathroom, after eating hotdogs we had sex. It was very spontaneous and hot.

Mia and I stayed together over the next year and became close and there I was in in my final year of

FREDERICK LEE TOOMER

Russel Sage with my teenage love

CHAPTER 5

THE BIRTH OF A HU$TLER

My cousin's name was BB, the son of Bishop Jackson who died. BB was my mother's favorite nephew. He would come up from time to time and stay with us.

BB loved New York City. He was from Statesville North Carolina. He lived with his sister Hilary and his grandparents. His mother's name was Sheela. He would be another victim to the crack epidemic but not as an addict but to the flash in the cash. I was in my last year of Russell Sage.

BB use to come up quite frequently with his Caucasian girlfriend, Amber. My mother and father use to let them stay with us in our cramped up two-bedroom apartment. They slept in the living room where I slept. As a result, my mother always felt sorry for him from what happened to his father. Even though it was cramped up, it was cool having my older cousin.

There, we use to sit around and watch New Jack city where Wesley Snipes played Nino Brown, a ruthless drug kingpin from uptown New York city. The movie captured the crack epidemic of the eighties. BB and I would sit to watch this movie and idolize Nino Brown.

We would fantasize about being drug kingpins. Until that point, I never sold any drugs, yet I was just fascinated about the money and power it came with.

Being a kingpin, however, you must be an extremely ruthless person to be in the drug business. I would never forget my first-time selling drugs.

I met this guy; his name was Too. For some time, he was trying to recruit me into his drug crew called MFD. I would meet up with him on his block and we would proceed to Guy Brewer Blvd.

We finally arrived at the Blvd where he introduced me to another drug dealer named Sheen. These were real street guys more than I could ever be at the time in my life.

Deep down, I was scared and nervous. I really didn't know what to expect. Another part of me was excited!

Guy Brewer Blvd was an open drug market for crack, heroin, cocaine, etc. Rumors on the street showed the Blvd was grossing over a hundred thousand dollars a day. There were drug dealers standing on every inch of the corner.

At first, I couldn't believe what I was seeing than reality hit me. Wow Fred! You are surrounded by a bunch of criminals. Sheen handed me some yellow bundles of Heroine. He told me it was ten in the bundle, and they were eleven dollars apiece.

At first, I was a little confused, however, it was graduation time!

There was a dealer there that was above Sheen that supplied him the dope. He said to Sheen, does your man know what the fuck he is doing? I had to learn quickly. This was the streets. One mistake could cost you your life or freedom.

As the night went on, Too left. I stayed there with Sheen who broke down the situation for me. I observed and learned for the rest of the night. When the night was over, I told him I didn't have any place to go, and he said to me, "if I had room, you could stay with me" Unfortunately, he didn't. This was going to be a long night. Going back home wasn't an option. I ended up walking and riding the E train all night.

When I got back to the Blvd that morning, Sheen was standing right there. He said to me, "you are here early, looks like you're ready to make some money." I replied, "yes I'm ready." Sheen handed me the dope and told me to stash it under the phonebooth. It was my first time in the streets, and I would need his assistance to show me the quick hustle moves of the slums!

Sheen said, "stash it good"! Do you know how much time we can get if they find it? Sheen showed me how to stash it quickly! After a brief time of standing there, the undercover cops jumped out on us, threw us both against the wall and one told me "Your breath smells like pussy." They searched us but they didn't find the dope—Sheen had hidden!

Wow, that was close!

Sheen said to me, let us walk-off. We ended up walking to South Road where we met up with Too and other kids from the neighborhood. We went to forty-eight park to kill some time where a lot of the kids from my neighborhood would come to play basketball. I just stood there talking to a neighborhood friend named Herbie. As I was talking to him, my father pops up!

Herbie said to me, if you want, I can have him jumped! I said "no." I did not hate him and never wanted to see him hurt. When my father saw me, he looked mad. However, he also looked concerned. I would never forget that looked he had on his face. I knew my mother and father were very fed up with me. I was always in trouble. If I was not getting suspended, I was always in a fight. I was becoming a problem teenager.

By this time, no more belts. Rather, he would mentally and physically abuse me. He would call me retarded and punch me and tell me to go in the hallway. He would tell me to stay away from my sisters because I am a bum and no good, and he did not want them to turn out like me.

At one point, I started to believe that I was and maybe I did belong on the streets. I was just looking for my next opportunity to run away. I hated everything around me and even myself from living in poverty, feeling that I would never have or be anything. It was a feeling of self-hatred at the time, and I did not know how to combat that feeling.

It was almost the end of the school year. Too and I would get into an awfully bad argument. There was a kid that use to hang out with me on my block. He was also Kool with Too. Oh, my big mouth, I must have said something, and I do not remember exactly what it was. It was enough for Too where he wanted, to hurt me.

One day after school, I walked over to Waltham Street where Too and his crew would hang out. I saw Too, he jumped in my face, talking about how I doubled crossed him. He told his man Darren, to fight me. He was no match for me. I knocked him right on the fucking ground! His crew didn't try to jump me, and he didn't try to fight me. He knew he would have a fight on his hands, after that, they had to respect me.

After that situation, I just stayed away from his block even though Herbie had lived on the same block as Too. Herbie use to tell me all the time to come through and hang out, that the beef was over. It did not matter; it was time for me to move on. I did not want to be part of Too and his crew anymore. I just wanted to be independent and do my own thing. It was June and graduation time was coming.

I would have one more meeting with my guidance counselor, Mr. Ross. In the meeting, we talked about my next Hight school. Next, I was zoned for Andrew Jackson Hight School located in Cambria Heights in Queens. He also told me he could pull some strings and get me into Forest Hills Hight School. It was rated one of the top Hight Schools in Queens. My father's sister graduated there and years later became a lawyer.

He also told me he could get me into a business program, and I would have another mainstream class which would be Social Studies. He made me promise not to mess it up. And I had every intention to do the right thing, I really wanted this opportunity. I promised him I would not. I felt maybe this could eventually get me out the ghetto the right way.

By June, I graduated, and that was it for Russell Sage. As for all my friends I knew for years, it was time for me to leave them behind. It was an emotional time for me because, here I grew up and met my first girlfriend and made so many different friends. I was an extremely popular kid. However, it was time for this journey to come to an end and say goodbye to Russell Sage.

I will never forget my experiences. It was now graduation time!

CHAPTER 6
GRADUATION TIME

It was the summer of 1992. I just graduated from Russell Sage.

My relationship with Mia took a negative turn. It wasn't the same anymore. Her cousin told me she had another boyfriend and Mia denied it. However, we were both young and curious. Our teenage love started to fade away.

BB in Amber was supposed to come up and live with us that summer. One wrong choice can change our life forever and that's what happened to me. August of that summer, I was supposed to go to North Carolina with him and help him move back to New York. They were living in a small apartment in Statesville.

BB and I drove down to North Carolina in his Pontiac Grand Prix. He made a long ride seem quick. When we got there, I stayed with him in his apartment. When we arrived in North Carolina, he introduced me to everybody, and everybody liked him. BB knew all the top drug dealers and crack fiends.

He took me to a big house called the mansion

owned by Rich Day. He was one of the biggest hustlers in the town and all the drug dealers hung there. It was cool hanging out with him in his apartment. I felt very independent. It felt good to get out of the neighborhood for a while.

BB introduced me to this Caucasian girl. Her name was Gin, a friend of Amber's. Gin was built like a Black girl with dirty blond hair. I would never forget this girl. She would come and hang out with me while I was there.

I was really attracted to Gin and was ready to experience other girls in was curious about white women. BB and I would talk about selling crack in North Carolina. He used to brag about how much money he's seen crack dealers make. It seemed like it was a fantastic opportunity to make money. However, years later I would realize how unorganized and silly we were.

When we got there, I gave him fifty dollars. He put the other fifty and we set up shop in his apartment. We started buying a hundred-dollar slabs of crack worth two hundred dollars on the street. BB knew all the white fiends that love to smoke crack.

The money was flowing quickly!

We needed more products so we could increase sales. We only had two weeks in his apartment then the lease was up, and we had to leave. Not much time to make any real money. We talked about if things worked out, we would come back down.

Before I knew it, two weeks was up, and it was time to leave. Gin would spend the last night with me. I wanted her so bad. Gin had a reputation as a fast white girl. I was hoping she would be fast with me. We kissed and played with each other all night. Well, that's all we would do.

The next day, we exchanged numbers. BB and I were on our way back to New York. That day I got back, I had to go to Forest Hills. This was going to be the toughest times in my life up until that point; things began to change for me. The events that happen would be like a domino effect and change my life forever.

That day, I went to Forest Hills to pick up my schedule. I could remember for the first-time walking into Forest Hills.

I said to myself, "wow, I made it this far" and I couldn't believe how many kids they were.

I went to my assigned homeroom and picked up my schedule. I said to myself again, "wow, I only have three years left, this is my opportunity to change my life."

I only recognized one kid I knew from Russell Sage; I didn't know anyone else I saw there.

I left with excitement in my belly! I couldn't wait to get there the next day. When I got back home later that day, my father and mother and BB were waiting for me.

My father said to me, "I found this letter in your room." I said to myself, wow, I can't believe I forgot something like that!

I couldn't understand why he would be going through my personal belongings. Why? I was furious!

My father said to me, "you have been smoking crack with Gene"—one of my friends I attended Russell Sage with.

Up until that point, I can honestly say I smoked some weed with Sharper one time in my life. I never even thought about smoking crack. If you were a crack head back then, you got no respect and you could not hide it!

I never stole anything from him. I was never arrested for anything, Now, I am a lowlife crack head. My father then pulled out the letter I was writing to Mia, it said that I was smoking crack. What exactly happened was; one of the letters was misspelled, it was supposed to say selling crack.

However, I tried to correct the spelling but selling ended up looking like smoking. My father said to me you are going to a drug rehab. So, my mother and father put me in the car and took me to J cap. It was a drug rehab program.

When we got there, the drug counselor asked my father, "is there any way we can solve this problem from my home?" My father immediately said "No"! The counselor knew deep down when he looked at me, I was not and hardcore crack addict.

I genuinely believed back then my father's life was so fucked up He wanted to destroy mine and I tried to fight them tooth and nail.

The sad thing is, do you think my cousin said

anything to try to help me? They ended up taking me to an inpatient drug rehab called J cap on liberty avenue in South Jamaica.

Everything went down the drain for me. The promise I made to Mr. Ross ended up being a broken promise. The business program also went down the drain.

In all… because of a stupid letter and father that seem like he hated me deep down! I did not know where I was going from there. All I knew was, I was filled with hate and embarrassment. Instead of attending high-school, I would be attending drug groups with people with real drug problems and mental issues.

From this point on, the cap would be my new residence.

CHAPTER 7
WELCOME TO J CAP

I can remember my first day walking into J cap. There were people everywhere. There was this big meeting room where the whole house had to meet.

Up the hall, there were men and women dorms where everybody slept. It was a big cafeteria where we would eat breakfast, lunch, and dinner. The People surrounded me was much older than I was. It was like, I was sixteen going on thirty.

I remember the first night being the hardest. I would meet a guy name Ripton Bell who helped me get adjusted. Ripton Bell slept on the bunk next to mine.

The first night was the roughest being that I was sleeping around a bunch of strangers. I would hear men screaming all night, trying to fight their Heroine urges.

I know from my trip with it a Heroin addiction is extremely hard to kick. It was the first time I witnessed first-hand what the drug can exactly do to you. In here, I was in this place living a lie and had no drug problem at all. In all reality, I could not relate to what these people were going through.

What made it worse, I was not mandated there like a lot of them. So, I could leave anytime I wanted to. But if I left, where was I going to go? All I could think about was, I wish I were in Forest Hills.

I felt like the loneliest kid in the world who have been stripped of everything that meant something to me. Every day I got up; I was always depressed. We were not allowed any television or contact with the outside world.

It was a change to what I thought life would be if I never came here. Our daily routines around the house would include attending daily groups.

With the freedom I had experienced while outside, this new life was becoming so boring for me. With no choice, I had to get along.

We would form a circle of people sitting in chairs and we would discuss all different types of topics. I would hear all types of stories about how drugs destroyed these people's lives.

I heard crazy stories about a guy so strung out on drugs that he put a baby in a microwave. He cried while telling this story. Mostly all the group could not understand his motive. There was another man that revealed his prison stories. He talked about being brutally raped in prison and how that made him rape other men.

All these stories I would hear, I never thought drugs could have such a negative impact on people's lives. The women's stories were even worse. They would talk about how drugs destroyed their lives and how their children were taken away, and how they were fighting to get their children back. I was in the cap for about thirty days.

I haven't spoken to my family or had any outside contact. When the thirty days were up, they transferred me to another facility they had in St Albans located by Roy Wilkins Park. When I arrived there, they put me in a room with three other guys. One of the guys was the same age as me. His name was Roger Hubby.

He was mandated there for probation. Roger Hubby was from Rochdale located by the facility. Roger and I got along simply fine. There was another guy named Ray Crag. He was from the Springfield gardens area where my father used to take me to service customers.

Crack would make its way into this beautiful Black middle-class neighborhood in Laurelton Queens. And destroy Black middle-class families.

Ray use to brag about a drug crew led by Tony Montana. His real name was Thomas Mickens, who ran the Springfield Garden drug crew and later convicted for tax evasion.

By that time, the feds came in and locked up all the top drug kingpins. Fat Cat and his top associate, Pappy Mason were locked up for the murder of rookie police officer Edward Burns, which happened right around the corner from where I lived. The police turned one of the houses into a police house and many years later rookie cop

Edward Burns got a street named after him.

They also took down Kenneth McGriff, better known as Supreme on the streets. In 1989, he pleaded guilty to running a continued criminal enterprise. He was sentenced to twelve years and eventually convicted, serving a life sentence for murder.

It was the end of an era for some South Jamaica drug lords. The crack thirsty streets of South Jamaica would change hands to a different generation of hustlers. As I settled into the St Albans facility, it was a little more comfortable. J Cap had its daily house functions.

The whole purpose of a drug rehab program is to put a structure in your life.

These places are usually run with a lot of military tactics. J cap had a chain in command set up just like the military. The residents ran the whole house. The counselors oversaw the house manager was responsible for the chain in command. This was the daily functions of the house.

As time pass on, the cap had a day called a family day where your family was allowed to visit to see if you were making any progress. This was a day to see my family again.

My mother came down and brought my two sisters. It was a very emotional visit. I didn't realize how much I missed them until they had to leave. I had tears in my eyes when they left. It was now October; I was admitted there in September.

My mother would make a push for me to come out. She started to dislike the program's policies. I had an accident there where I stepped on a nail and had to go to the hospital. She was upset that the cap never contacted her.

One day, my mother and father came up there and signed me out. This gave me immense joy and relieve. Thank God, I was finally out of the cap. When I got out, we weren't living in South Jamaica anymore. We were now living in Springfield Gardens. They rented a three-bedroom apartment, and I shared a room with my younger brother Robby.

When I got there, they threatened me to tell them everything I and BB were doing down south, or they would send me back. I told them everything that happened in North Carolina. They told me I would have to attend an outpatient drug program. I wanted to go back to school; however, they felt that me going to a drug program was more important.

I was going to turn seventeen in a couple of months. I was a high school drop out with no income, no real future ahead of me and a dysfunctional family. It wasn't easy for me. I had to deal with all these problems. My father let me work for him on weekends.

I contacted Mia, perhaps we would see each other one more time. However, things weren't the same between us. Eventually, we would call it quits. Life had changed, everything had changed.

It was time for us to go our separate ways. At first, it was hard for me to accept. However, I knew we might have been better off that way.

My life had made a U-turn and Mia was doing very well in school.

Moving forward, I didn't have any friends. Sharper and I would lose touch. The next and last time I would see him would be three years later on Jamaica avenue in Queens. BB would go back to North Carolina and join the Navy. I wouldn't see him again until years later.

At that point, I was in the pimp game. He would drive me to the track in Queensbridge to check out my new hustle. I knew at some point in my life the truth would come out that I never had a drug problem. It wouldn't matter because no one would believe me.

Deep down, I hated living with this lie. The worse thing was the lie never helped me. Rather, it destroyed my life. I would never know how it feels to ask a girl to the prom or try out for any high school sports teams or just graduate high school. I knew from that point on, life would be a tuff mountain to climb.

The repercussions of what I put myself in I would have to learn to live with. The bottom line: it was time for me to really grow up.

My next journey would be Away out.

Onward, I would start to mature as a young man and learn the New York city rat race.

CHAPTER 8

BECOMING A SALESMAN

Awayout would become my next journey.

My parents and I agreed if I attended Awayout outpatient drug program I could come home. I really didn't have a choice, so I agreed. Awayout was in Long Island city in Queens.

My mother stood by me as much as she could. I knew deep down she cared, and she wanted the best for me.

My mother came with me the first day when I was admitted. I was only seventeen, so my mother still had to sign for me.

My father was the one who put me in there and he was unable to drive us. My mother and I had to take the train.

When we got there, my mother asked some questions, signed the papers, and there I was in another drug program. Awayout ran under the same guidelines J cap did.

You have a house structure ran by the house manager and the counselors overseeing the house. They assigned me to a drug counselor, Kathy Sokols. She was an extremely attractive middle-aged Greek woman who had a son about my age.

I liked Kathy; she was like Ms. Bullock. She had this mother nurturing about herself. Kathy and I would meet each week and whatever issues I had; I was able to talk about. In order to graduate from the program, they sent me to therapy around the Woodside area in Queen's. It cost me forty-five dollars for a weekly visit. I would commute every day from Springfield gardens, get off at twenty-third and Ely Avenue and walk down to Awayout. We had to be there every day—Monday to Friday at 9:00AM.

When we got there in the morning, we would all stand around in a circle and recite the serenity prayer.

This would start the mornings off. I would meet a lot of different people who attended Awayout.

I remember meeting a guy named Cedric. He was about my father's age and a great basketball player like my father. Cedric in some diverse ways reminded me of him. He was a big guy just like my pops; six feet over two hundred pounds. He became the older brother I never had.

Cedrick was mandated there from an upstate prison in New York.

I could remember him being the first person to take me to money-making; Manhattan and to the legendary forty-second street peepshows.

It was the first time I would see so many different sexy naked women. It was the experience of a lifetime as a young man.

Cedrick always gave me great advice. He would tell me, "To achieve anything, you have to be able to see it, believe it, then achieve it." Those words of inspiration stayed with me a lifetime. I saw Cedric fight his addiction like a heavyweight champion in the ring. When we all graduated that year ending, I knew he really deserved it.

Now, the test is to stay clean and just very few can. This was a lifetime addiction. Years later when Ms. cocaine came in my life, I could finally relate to what Cedric was going through.

I could remember this young pretty phone girl named Regina. Regina and I had an instant attraction for each other. One day, we ended up kissing each other and from that point on she became my girlfriend. I met this real sexy Latin girl there. Her name was Ruby. She was friends with another girl's mother who was a client there.

Ruby was so beautiful; she had these gorgeous eyes and a killer body.

As I think back about Ruby, I remember the times walking her home in Astoria Queens.

The attention this beautiful sexy young Latin girl use to get was alarming. Every man would always stop to look at her, she was irresistible.

After meeting Ruby, I broke it off with Regina. If I had understood the pimp game as I did years later, Ruby and Regina would have been perfect candidates. I knew in my heart Regina would have been the better girlfriend.

However, I was caught up in Ruby's looks. One day, Ruby and I was sitting in the park and guess who pops up with their girlfriend: Regina and her friend. They act like they wanted to fight the girl! I must admit I was a little nervous. I just sat there and listened. She asked her how long Ruby and I were seeing each other? Ruby replies in her soft sexy Latino voice not long. Then Regina sadly and quickly walked off with her friend.

This was the last time I saw Regina. Sad thing is, Regina was the better choice, but I fell for Ruby's Latino sex appeal! I lost them both in the end. Ruby and I never took off.

The year at Awayout, I wanted to accomplish three things: first, get my high school equivalency diploma; second, driver's license and third, graduate Awayout. I did achieve two out of the three goals. I got my driver's license and for my equivalency diploma, I missed it by failing one subject which was Math and later that year, I did graduate Awayout.

When I graduated, I didn't feel like I accomplished anything because I didn't have a drug problem. After the graduation, Cedric and I parted ways. He was supposed to start driving trucks. He contacted me one day and wanted me to go to a drug rehab meeting with him, but I couldn't relate to his drug problem.

Eventually, it was time for Cedric and me to lose touch.

I had learnt sometimes years later, running into

Tony Trip who knew me from Awayout. Rumor was Cedrick's addiction had gotten the best of him. He ended up back upstate.

My father was on my case all the time about when I turned eighteen years old. I had to move out.

I remember looking through the newspaper for jobs and found this ad: warehouses workers needed to hire immediately! The ad said they were located on three-fifty Coney Island Avenue in Brooklyn.

I took the F train to Brooklyn, got off at Coney Island Avenue and there I was. I remember while walking in there, I heard loud music playing. There was an extremely high energetic feeling about this place.

There was this man who came out and introduced himself as Stan. He was one of the four managers who ran the place. He was very friendly and direct.

Stan took me into this room where they were having morning sales meetings and they were yelling "juice! juice!" There was also a man in there pumping these guys up to go out there and sell products.

Even though the ad was misleading, I was very intrigued. I always wanted to know how to sell. When you are an entrepreneur, you must be able to put your sales hat on—its prevalent. Sales is the bloodline and the survival of any business.

In my mind, even if things did not work out,

I would learn the sales game and maybe pick up some business moves along the way. Stan introduced me to everybody in the place. He introduced me to his Partner Pay. Pay and Stan ran the clearance division; Donnie and Devin ran the fashion division. They all got promoted from the Staten Island office.

Basically, this was a direct marketing company with a pyramid scheme. Stan told me he would be the one who was training me and taking me out to the field. This would be my first day!

Stan drove us to Ocean's Avenue in Brooklyn. It was a very high retail area and I watched everything Stan did. He parked his car, filled his box up with his products and we started on with our business and pitching our products. We were selling these calculators for ten and these body massagers for eight dollars.

As we would hit business after business, we would hear stuff like "no I'm not interested" or "got it already" or just plain "no." Stan was a good hustler and salesman that knew how to hustle pass all the rejections until he heard the yes. Stan would tell me it's a numbers game and the more people you can see, the better your chances are.

I learned a lot from Stan.

I had seen him gross over two hundred dollars that day. Once I had seen that, the thoughts that went through my mind told me, I better take a shot any way; what did I have to lose? I was young and willing to give anything a chance. The messenger job I started out with didn't work out. In Manhattan, one day, I ran into a delivery truck in the middle of midtown Manhattan. Henceforth, I decided bike messenger wasn't for me!

I told Stan I would see him the next day when we got back to the office. Stan introduced me to another salesperson; his name was Sonny Nelson. A young white Irish kid that lived on green street in the neighborhood. Sonny and I would hang out every day after work and drink beer and smoke weed. We were young guys with no real responsibilities.

All we ever thought about was just to have fun. Sonny had no hang-ups because I was Black. He always made me feel comfortable around him. One day after work, I ate dinner with his mother and father. They made me feel like family. I felt welcomed and his family was becoming my second family.

Sonny and I became like Laurel and Hardy after a while. We teamed up with each other. We both wanted to get into our own office, so it made sense for us to hook up.

The next day, I came back with a sales vengeance in my eyes and ready to work. Pay Stan's partner took me out and then he let me try on my own. I made a hundred dollars that day.

I was extremely motivated about my current sales job. I told my mother and father and of course my father knocked it. He knocked everything I wanted to do. It didn't matter though. I was the person who didn't have a high school diploma.

I was willing to try anything at the time, so, I still worked with my father on the weekends. Sonny and I would team up with this other guy; his name was Joey Copco. He was in from San Jose California. His family was originally from Bensonhurst. That's where his grandparents lived on new Utrecht Avenue in Brooklyn.

Joey would hang with I and Sonny every night. I always had the best times of my life with these two guys. I can honestly say, some of the best times in my life I had, were with Sonny and Joey. we were becoming the three stooges.

We would all pop acid together, get drunk, stay up late and chase women. We all went to the first historical Summer Jam concert in June of ninety-five where we watched acts like Notorious Big, Wu Tang Clan, Shaba Ranks, Brandy, Naughty by Nature, etc., they all put on great performances. We were all in the clearance division.

I still remember Donnie and Devin. They started selling this bootlegged merchandise. They always sent the guys out with this merchandise, and this was against impulse policies.

Eventually, Stan wanted to get into the action, Pay didn't. However, he got dragged in, they were making a lot of money off these bootlegged shirts t-shirts jackets and hats. It was too much money involved to say no. This had gone on for some time.

Then, I remember coming back from the field one day and it was a new guy there from the head office. The numbers had dropped substantially. The office was moving more of bootlegged products than impulses.

They sent him down to retrain all the managers in the office. Stan left immediately he started working with the Italians in Bensonhurst. Stan was known as a straight businessman. He told everyone if they still wanted to collaborate with him to come to Bensonhurst and he would still set you up in your own deal.

I knew deep down it was never going to be any deal with Stan—he was selling game. I went down to Stans new office in Bensonhurst. He introduced me to his new partners. Believe me, these wasn't your regular salesman. I don't think these guys would be able to accept their merchandise coming up lost. That would be the last time I would go to Stans office.

Stan just needed people to move his bootleg merchandise. He truly had no intention of putting anyone in their own office. At impulse, Sonny wanted to jump ship to the fashion division. He thought Donnie and Devin would be the coolest guys to work for.

The only reason why I teamed up with Sonny was because I thought I would have a better shot moving up the pyramid. I really thought Sonny wanting to jump ship was a bad idea.

We were the first crew on in the clearance division.

In each division there, first year in business

was responsible to push out at least one deal. In business, it's not about if you like or love; just get that nonsense out of your head. It's about making the best business decisions for yourself regardless of the situation.

Of course, the situation with Donnie and Devin didn't work. Year ending, Sonny left the business. Joey moved back to Piscataway, New Jersey with his father. Sonny always said, after a year and nothing works out, he would leave the business.

The deal went bad for me. I would eventually figure out where the wholesale bootlegged spots were in money-making Manhattan. Essentially, it turned into a nice sideline hustle to have with not having to answer to a boss. I would buy my products wholesale and hustle different spots around New York City. In the end, I didn't make it into my own office.

However, I did become a salesman and picked up some important business tactics.

Most of all, I made friends and have memories that would last a lifetime.

CHAPTER 9
THE WONDER YEARS

The year was 1995. Hip-hop music was on the rise, and in the next two years two of Hip-hop's biggest legends would die. I was nineteen years old when Tupac died and a year later his east coast rival Biggie Smalls would die to. Both would be killed on the west coast. To this day their murders are still unsolved. The President of the United States was Bill Clinton. The Mayor of New York city was Rudy Giuliani and the richest man in the world was Bill Gates.

The most powerful company was General Motors and our nation's unemployment rate was at 5.4%. I was in search of an opportunity that would lead me to job security. How many people do you know who really likes their job? How many of us are forced into believing that a job defines who we are?

In 1995, I was getting ready to start my first full-time job at Wonder Bread located in Jamaica Queens on Douglass Avenue. My mother helped me get the job from one of my father's customers. His name was Aryl. He had a twin brother named

Ronald who worked for Wonder Bread. What do our parents teach us about job security and money when we are young?

Most parents do not teach their children the difference between the money trap in the money game. Get a good job and stay there and retire in collect a pension. This way of thinking at one point would be obsolete. Having a job does not mean you understand money. It just means you work for money.

As young Black kids, we are taught to work for money. We are not taught to have money work for us. This is the number one reason we start out in life behind the eighth ball.

What's taught to us as children decides our outcome as adults. The reality is job security, which is false security.

The system is all set up for us to work all our life and drop dead before we can collect anything. At the average ages being sixty-two and sixty-five years old.

Hopefully, you do not get any real sickness. The working man's intellect must be versatile. Times were changing from the industrial age to the information age. I met with the head of the shipping department. His name was Jack Wilson. He was a real cool boss who hired me immediately. I started at Wonder Bread in March of 1995.

It was told to me by the rest of the union guys, if I worked thirty days straight, I could make the union. With the help of Aryl keeping me on the schedule, I made the thirty days straight. Wonder Bread, in the beginning, I would mostly come in on the graveyard shift. I would fill in for guys who were on vacation or guys that called in sick.

The weekends hanging out with Sonny, I noticed he knew everybody in his neighborhood that smoked marijuana. Up until that point, I never sold any marijuana. I was willing to give it a shot even though I had a job now. My plan was to make as much money as I could from my job or from creating a sideline hustle. Now, let's face it!

As a working individual, you must be able to try other ventures, or you will always fall victim to a time clock. I was very ambitious and young and curious about becoming financially free. Sonny and I discussed becoming partners.

Remember, you learn more from your mistakes as opposed to when everything is in your favor. In life and business, it's all about learning how to deal with adversity because success in life is not a negotiation. It doesn't talk to you; it doesn't pick you. You must be able to shit piss it, live it, and die it! It must be a full part of you, or you will never achieve it!

Sonny and I brought in Don as a third partner. We all put six hundred dollars apiece. I knew nobody at that time I could buy a pound of weed from. I let Sonny and Don handle that part.

I remember Sonny calling me at my place in Queens and telling me he's got it! I went to Brooklyn immediately that day and met Sonny at his apartment.

When I walked into the kitchen, this was the first time I ever have seen a pound of weed. The smell of this big fluffy green plant lingered through the whole apartment. Sonny said to me, "do you want to smoke son?" I said, "hell yeah, roll it up"!

The funny thing was, I didn't even know how to roll weed up and there it was a pound sitting right in front of my face.

As we started smoking, after a couple of pulls, I felt the immediate intensity from the weed. And I asked him, "what is the name of this weed?? He replied, "red hair son," with excitement! So, we had paid six hundred dollars each for a pound of red hair. The plan was for everybody to take their share which would be five ounces apiece and we were all responsible to bring back our share so we can re-up on the next pound.

My plan was to take it to my job. I knew some people who smoked. However, I didn't have a real customer base like I knew Sonny and Don did. I brought a couple of hustlers in, whom I knew, to help me move it. I knew this hustler on the job. His name was Erick, an underground rapper, and a stone-cold hustler.

I also brought in my cousin, Amos. He lived down the block from me on Southgate Street. Amos was a lousy hustler and a little stupid. He messed up the ounce I gave him.

He was a big waste of time, but Erick paid up

immediately the first time.

I was already losing money. Sonny was doing better than I was in Brooklyn. The second time around, Don came through for us again. We paid fifteen hundred dollars for this pound. We split it up as planned and I took mine back to Queen's with me. I moved it.

However, my hustle wasn't on point. I thought maybe I could get a couple of guys I knew to help build my business, but it turned into a disaster. Erick told me he was taking to many shorts, and he wanted to get back into the cocaine business.

I couldn't do business with Amos anymore and my end was moving slow.

How could I go back to Sonny and tell him on my end things wasn't working out? I took the money from my paycheck to cover the short money, so we could buy the next pound. This time, it was time for us to re-up on our product.

Sonny and Don couldn't find a supplier, so this was my turn to find one. I ran into an old junior high school friend I knew named Gene. He knew all the Jamaican weed dealers in the Bronx.

He introduced me to a guy named Tommy who lived in the South Bronx. Sonny and Don gave me the whole Fifteen hundred dollars and I went to the South Bronx the next morning. I met with Tommy, and I bought a pound of skunk for a thousand dollars, way cheaper than the prices they were getting in Brooklyn. I took it back to Brooklyn and we split it up.

However, I had decided this would be my last purchase. I realized some mistakes I made and what it takes to be successful in this business, so I told Sonny and Don they were on their own after this. They were facing their issues on their end as well.

I had learned a lot with this marijuana hustle and decided it would become my secondary hustle in time to come.

Talking about my family, it had its own issues. My father was in overdue tax trouble with Uncle Sam. My mother met a young man named Joe Brooks from North Carolina who worked in a sneaker store.

Joe was expecting an inheritance. It stipulated he had to move out his mother's house to receive it. My father agreed to let Joe stay there. It was just one catch.

Joe couldn't know that my mother and father were married. My sisters and I had to call him Uncle Mike. I knew sooner or later this would break our family apart.

It was time for me to look for somewhere else to go. I hated that we had to call my father Uncle Mike. I didn't like Joe, my mother's new friend very much and I don't think my father did either.

The first opportunity I would get, I would move out! And job security would be my only hope now.

CHAPTER 10

A QUEENS ROMANCE

Wonder Bread became a way of life for me.

I was there almost eight months. My life was changing.

I could remember as a young man, I use to get on the E train and get off at Roosevelt Avenue in Queens.

There were a bunch of Columbian brothels in the neighborhood. I didn't have any steady girlfriend at the time, so occasionally, I would pay the brothels a visit.

I had always loved Latin women, especially the real slutty-sexy type. At Wonder Bread, I got friendly with a guy named Messiah who worked on the shipping dock. We used to hang out after work and drink beers.

Messiah used to tell me all the time about this woman named Sasha, who was good friends with his girlfriend, Nita. He used to brag about how fine she was and how bad he wanted sexual relations with her.

I can remember one Sunday after a long work week I was in Springfield gardens relaxing.

Suddenly, I heard the doorbell.

I went downstairs, it was Messiah with excitement in his voice, he said "She's here…! She's here…!" as he kept repeating.

I had always said to myself, what if I never answered the door because this walk was going to change my life forever. I said to Messiah, "okay I'll go," and we proceeded on a Fifteen-minute walk to Rochdale.

When we got there, Nita answered the door. She said, hi Fred. I greeted her in a casual manner, and there was Sasha who was right there making up the couch. Messiah introduces us and we greeted each other with curiosity.

She looked me over quick and then she said to me, "this was not the best time for us to meet." I said, "okay."

I couldn't help but notice her sexy big chest and her black homegirl swag. I was hooked instantly! Sasha was a short sexy woman with these sexy mysterious eyes that could attract any man.

She was much older than me but, I didn't care.

I told her OKAY. We exchanged numbers and I left with an erotic picture of her in my head. The next weeks, Sasha and I would talk to each other on the phone. I enjoyed our conversations and anticipated the next time we would talk.

At the time I met Sasha, I was in the process of looking for my own place. I kept telling my mother I was tired of stepping on my brothers' toys every night and it was time for me to move. My mother being who she is, found a place down the street and told me she talked to the guy who was renting the room and she looked at it.

The same week, I went in, looked at the place and met the man who was renting it. His name was Mr. Allan Robinson.

He lived there with his mother, his younger son Allen junior, his other family members. His nephew, a playground legend and future N-B-A superstar who also lived there with his mother. Mr. Allan and his mother were originally from Harlem New York. It was rumored he was one of the biggest pimps Harlem had ever seen back in the days.

I didn't know at the time he would become my mentor and best friend and teach me the cold-blooded pimp game. Mr. Allan showed me the second-floor apartment. It was perfect for me. He told me it was a hundred and twenty-five dollars a week. And if he sees anybody after five days it's going to cost me an extra twenty-five dollars. I gave him two weeks upfront and he gave me the keys and there I was in my first place.

That night, I talked to Sasha and told her about it, and we agreed to meet each other in a week's time. I was so excited to get my own place. I did what a poor person would do. I got all my furniture from rent a center.

I couldn't wait for Sasha's fine ass to come.

Our date was set for Friday night. I would never forget the night when Sasha and I would have our first date. I could remember that Friday like it was yesterday. I worked earlier that day.

When I got off, I just went back to my place and just chilled out and got ready for my night with Sasha. I could remember Erick dropping by that day. We smoked some killer weed.

As we were smoking, the phone rang. It was Sasha calling me to pick her up from Rochdale. I asked Erick to drop me off and he said yeah.

We left and proceeded to Rochdale. From the intense feeling from the weed, I was feeling good. When we got there, he dropped me off. I told him later and went up to Nita's apartment.

When I got there, Nita opens the door for me. Sasha was right there sitting on the couch with her hair done looking real pretty.

She had a mysterious look in her sexy cat eyes. I couldn't help it but notice she had looked like something was bothering her. I asked, "is anything wrong?" She said, "no." We stayed for a little while and talked to Nita then eventually we called a cab and left. When we got back to my place, Sasha made herself very comfortable.

She went into the kitchen, and she started making some spaghetti. I had told her through conversations on the phone that spaghetti was my favorite dish.

As Sasha started making the spaghetti, I rolled us some weed and poured us some Alize, putting on some slow jams as our two lonely souls sat there on the couch smoking and enjoying the romantic intensive feeling that was in the air.

As we looked into each other's eyes, and all that mattered was that we were not alone again. Even if it's only for one night. I would sit there and just listen to her talk about past relationships and her life.

We both started feeling a little bit tipsy from the alcohol and marijuana. I could sense the feeling that we both wanted each other that night. We looked deeply in each other eyes and started to kiss each other with a deep desire of lust.

I took my hands and rubbed her breast while we just kissed each other passionately. I laid Sasha on the bed and caressed her small voluptuous body nice and slow with my lips. I sucked on her big nipples very aggressively.

She would moan with pleasure.

Over here, I was in heaven as I would beg to taste her and she would open her legs, letting my tongue taste her hot juices.

She would close her eyes, pushing my head deeper in her wet trap.

Finally, I wanted to feel inside her wet kitty. She opened her legs and let me enter inside her wet experienced trap. I was in complete enjoyment.

After getting inside, I couldn't hold back. I exploded my white lust all over my sheets.

She said, "Fred," very abruptly, "that was too fast, you're going to have to do something about that!"

Sasha didn't know that was the first time I was

with a woman with such experience. After that night, the next morning, we would eat the leftover spaghetti we never touched.

Sasha left later that day and returned when I came back from work. Every time she came by, we would have very erotic sex, smoke weed and just relax. Even though we would get into silly arguments, I ended up falling in love with her.

Sasha started moving her stuff in little by little and after a while she was completely moved in. My mother hated Sasha. She said she was everything I didn't need in my life. Sasha was cool and maybe, she wasn't the best choice.

However, I wanted to spend all my time with her.

Sasha at the time lived with her mother and two sons. She also had two older brothers that lived there too. Her family was dysfunctional just like mine.

My sister Regina and my mother cursed Sasha out very bad on the phone and they threatened to fight her. I immediately stopped talking to them both. It was my choice if I wanted Sasha in my life or not.

This would turn me against my family for years. Sasha and I would grow closer to each other, and she would become everything to me.

We would start to do everything with each other. Not only did I fall in love with her, but she also became my best friend and partner in crime.

It was a Queens Romance!

CHAPTER 11
ARE YOU THE PIMP OR PROSTITUTE?

I almost had about a year in at Wonder Bread.

I was getting my degree, not in college, however. I was learning all aspects of business from the streets to how a corporation is ran; from how a product was manufactured and distributed because at Wonder Bread we did everything right there.

We produced and distributed the product to grocery stores and supermarkets all around New York city. I will never say I loved working at Wonder Bread because I never did. At one point, I wanted to break the chains of corporate slavery. I knew this information and experience I was gaining were priceless.

This wisdom could help me run my own business in the future. I told myself, I didn't want to get pimped my whole life.

What is a PIMP? POWER IN MANIPULATING PEOPLE!

There are pimps or pimping in all stages of life, from the biggest to lowest levels. The biggest corporations in the world are pimps.

Look at your tv commercials and advertisement around you. The average person who gets up to work every day only understands how to create debt which keeps corporations extremely profitable.

The average person who gets up to work every day they haven't made a choice on which category they belong to. There are only two choices: either you're in the money trap or the money game. It is either you're the pimp or the prostitute; the choice is yours.

Once we establish and understand which side of the coin we are on, we must be completely honest with ourselves about being the best prostitute we can be.

A good prostitute knows and understands their dedication to the game.

A good prostitute knows and understands she is getting pimped. She also knows I'm going to be a damn good prostitute and take control of my own soul.

Those early Africans that were forced into slavery were getting pimped. These Africans had no choice; it was always "nigga get in this boat or die!" This country was founded and built on pimping and on the backs of those early Africans.

The Rockefellers, the Kennedys, JP Morgan, etc., these people were masters of the unwritten rules to success. They were some of the biggest pimps this country has ever seen. The unwritten rules to success, what are they? Who makes these rules up?

I could remember working at Wonder Bread, I use to talk to all the senior guys who worked there twenty-plus years.

A lot of them, after all that time were still living paycheck to paycheck. Some were living way beyond their means.

Very few would say, "yeah I have been here for years, but when I retire, I'll have investments." Or "I own real estate" or "I have a nice stock portfolio." What I did hear a lot was: "I have to wait until I'm sixty-five so I can collect my pension and social security at the same time."

And some would say they might have to work part-time to make ends meet after they retire. Are you kidding me? Work after you retire.

At that point, work should be a voluntary option. Very few of these guys and I understood the money game. The sad thing is, in most Black families, capitalism isn't taught. Most of us including myself don't know what to do with money.

The money game is a lifetime relationship we are married to whether we like it or not. That is the bottom line!

My father had a decent example. His father did not believe in credit cards. He did not believe in creating debts. However, he did believe in good debt which is called assets. The building of which he owned and operated C.T exterminating.

He also rented out the storefront and received monthly rent in one of the most upscale Black neighborhoods in Queens. Back in the days, St Albans was home to some of the biggest Black entertainers: Count Basie, James Brown, Lena Horne and Miles Davis, the Black elite would have a true residence in St Albans for life. My grandparents William and Rosa lee Jackson had a house on Sullivan Road in St Albans where they raised my mother and seven other siblings I love going there when I was young passing the famous wall with all of those Black legends painted on it.

I decided at one point that I was not going to get pimped all my life. It was time to control my own soul. I decided to take some unconventional risks.

When I was younger, I never really understood why a woman would want to sell her body to different men for money. Society gives you a bad outlook when it comes to prostitutes and pimps.

I could remember when I was a kid looking at the prostitutes walk up and down the Atlantic City strip as my father was driving. I never thought years later I would have women working that same Atlantic city strip.

Sasha would come in my life and change everything forever. I could remember her brother use to ask Sasha if she could keep one of his new turnouts. Her name was Candy.

She was a seventeen young Trinidadian girl who her brother, Freaky had just copped. I used to tell Sasha, don't get involved, don't let her stay here! At the time I knew nothing about pimping, I was a straight square back then. I always let her get her way.

I knew in my heart; her brother was no good. This situation would only lead us into trouble. I could see she was interested in this business.

I was young at the time and couldn't see all the angles. I couldn't put my foot down and say no!

I guess, deep down, I was interested too.

Sasha came to me at one point and told me she wanted to get into the business. With my own curiosity I agreed.

We were just two hustlers from Queens who saw an easy way to make money. The questions that rolled through my mind was, "how do you get a whore?"

The reality was how do I learn the art of the pimp game. Pimping is an art and yes, you have a lot of pimps.

Master pimps are rare! As my mentor use to tell me, you have A and B in everything: Lawyers, Authors, and businesspeople. In these professions, there is always someone who is the best out of everybody.

The same thing with pimps. You have masters and you have the amateurs. It's a life of flash in cash. However, it's not for every cat.

Understanding that Sasha wanted to be a part of this business made me always question myself, "what type of woman do I really have?"

Maybe, she wanted to be a whore and my square ass could not turn her out. This business would come to me like a thief in the night. I could not find this business when I was single. It had to come to me when I found someone I cared about.

I had just learned she was pregnant with my first and only child. Also, Sasha's brother, Freaky would eventually get arrested and sent back upstate.

Now, this was Sasha's opportunity to cop two of her brother's girls. She was over her mother's house when she spoke to her brother on the phone and told him Candy and Oreo decided to come with her.

We took them both back to the room. They were both young turnouts that could choose or leave any time you put them down, especially if a pimp's game is not wrapped tight and we were new to the game.

Sasha would take them both back to the room, she would fix both up and take them out to Queen's Bridge on a Friday night.

By this time, the legendary pimp game which was originally the Black man's street game had seen its golden days in the seventies and early eighties.

In the eighties, crack hit the scenes and turned most of your top pimps and whores to fiends. The game had changed hands to a younger generation of pimps that had no class. They wore sneakers and their pants hung from their ass.

The days of the well-dressed Pimp was over. Now, all you had was some old school Mack's trying to hang on to the past.

In long Island city, the same area where Awayout was located. All the pimps including her brother, Freaky use to take their whores and young turnouts out here to work. There would be tricks, driving around everywhere looking for whores.

When I first witnessed this, I felt like I was in a different world and yes, I was. The night Sasha took Candy and Oreo out, Oreo chose a pimp called Precious who served Sasha on the track. Candy ended up staying with us and I did not know anything about this business. I was still very intrigued; it was time for me to learn the pimp game.

What makes a woman a whore? How do you get them to bring you all their money?

These were questions and many more that started to roll through my mind.

If I was going to be a part of this world, I desperately needed to know the psychology behind it. I can remember one of the million-dollar questions was why does a hoe need a pimp? Well let me elaborate. Even if a whore is successful by herself. There is a certain type of mental an emotional stability that is needed for a woman especially in that line of work. In a square relationship a man should always be there to help his woman mentally. A square man cannot understand a whore and what they been through in their life for them to choose that lifestyle or what they go through on a daily basis. Whores need someone they can trust and depend on just as a square woman. A professional pimp has a deeper understanding of the business than an average man so he can identify with a whore on her level.

It was time for me to obtain an education on mind manipulation.

CHAPTER 12

A PIMPS COUPLE

October twenty-third, 1996, was the most important day in my life. This is the day my son, Fredrick Lee junior would come into this world.

This was the happiest day in my life.

I will never forget the day I was at Wonder Bread working the graveyard shift. Suddenly, the supervisor Aryl calls me and tells me somebody is on the phone for you. It was Sasha, calling me to come to Long Island Jewish hospital located in Elmhurst Queens New York.

As soon as I got the call, I was on my way to meet Sasha at the hospital. When I got there, they rushed me into the emergency room.

The nurses put the hair net over my head, and it was like Fred junior wasted no time coming in this world. It was the most amazing thing I have ever witnessed in my life, a natural childbirth. I could remember the first two people I called.

I called Sonny first but from the excitement in his voice, he was still too young to understand my enjoyment. I called my mother's house, and my father answered the phone. I told him about his first grandson coming into the world and he told me my mother said she did not want anything to do with me or the baby.

I was extremely hurt but I knew right there it was just Sasha and I and my new son and fuck everybody else! That same night, I had to take over for Sasha on the track. I was supposed to take Candy out to the bridge that night.

Candy was also pregnant working the track. Prostitution is like any other job. If your wife is a server, does she's stop going to work because she's pregnant? Neither does whores.

At this point, the income from Sasha's great hustling abilities, had accumulated us a nice three-thousand-dollar bankroll.

With the room becoming too small, Fred junior, Candy, and everybody else who stayed with us, it was time to move.

l remembered walking down Hillside Avenue in Jamaica Estates in Queens where I saw a sign apartment for rent. I went inside and inquired about the apartment. I asked them to show me the one-bedroom apartment.

As soon as I walked in, I said to myself this is perfect. A couple of days later, I brought Sasha back and showed her and she agreed.

Sasha and I moved in two weeks later. We gave Bonnie Lynn and realty one-month rent and one-month security which was fourteen hundred dollars.

In there, I was nineteen years old in my

new apartment with Sasha and my newborn son Fredrick Lee junior. Just to think, just three years ago, I was in junior high school, then a drug rehab. Things had turned around quickly.

She would turn this average one-bedroom apartment into an extremely beautiful luxurious apartment with stylish black ceilings, white wall paint job, twenty-eight hundred dollars black leather and sectional sixty-inch floor model tv. She really turned our new joint out! She had a true talent for decorating I was learning a lot from her being that she had ten years on me. Now I would get a taste of becoming a man.

We had a built-in bar that cost us three thousand dollars all together. Ten thousand dollars in brand new furnishings.

The crazy thing is, when you never had anything, you want that feeling of being rich. If I knew the money game, I would have invested that money.

At this point, we had the complete game to catch whores. We were still both squares. Our hustling routine worked like this: Sasha and her cousin in Candy would hit Queens Bridge every night. I would stay home, watch Fred, and rest up for work.

My woman or not, she was a hustler and I had to let her flow.

Sasha would make sure she was back before it was time for me to go to work. She was mentally getting turned out every night.

She went to Queen's Bridge watching those whores wearing those erotic outfits, jump in and out of those cars in the fast money she was hooked like a crook. I saw it every night in her cat eyes. The reality was, Candy really was not her girl. We were both new participants of this under ground world of pimps and whores. And of course, we couldn't see what was behind those devils' doors.

She did not really turn Candy out her brother did however, she gave her some style that made the tricks go wild. Candy only stayed as long as she did because they agreed to let Nita, Sasha's good friend at the time keep the baby.

In the pimp game, you must have leverage on a whore to keep her paying you as long as they can. Candy finally dropped that baby two months after Fred was born.

I remember all of us staying in our one-bedroom luxury apartment. I said to myself, if I am going to be in the pimp game, I will need a car.

I bought a brand new 1995 Mercury Mystique.

The car had like thirty-six thousand miles on it. I paid the sales tax of a thousand dollars and financed it for four hundred dollars a month.

This was a bad idea not getting the car. However, I should have never financed it. I should have bought a used car off the lot. That way, if things didn't work out with Candy, no big deal. I created extra debt in a one girl operation.

Whenever starting small in any business, you should keep expenses extremely low. Sasha and I paid a nanny to come to watch Fred at night and we both use to roll the track together. We were a pimps-couple.

The pimps use to laugh at us, and I got no respect of being a pimp because of the way the rest of the pimps felt—that Sasha should be out there too—and they pimped at her as well. And because of the way I turned out to the game as being a hustler not a traditional pimp who knew the rules of the game.

Although they didn't respect us, they still made their whores turn their heads when we drove by. I knew, being that no one was touching Candy, she was vulnerable to choose. Every whore wants to be touched they feel that's one of the reasons there paying a pimp. A real pimp doesn't get paid to get laid. A real pimp gets paid for understanding what to program in a whore's brain.

By the summertime, Candy's story was starting to heat up. At that time, we slept on Candy ambitions. This is the reason you must be five steps ahead of a whore. You can never think that everything is all right. At this point, we use to send Sasha's cousin out there with her. One early morning, I got a call from Sasha telling me Candy didn't return home with Couse in the morning. I left Wonder Bread immediately, went to the track, she was like a ghost.

I couldn't find her nowhere.

I returned home early that afternoon, the phone rings and it's Candy telling Sasha she chose some pimp named China who was back on the streets of Queens bridge looking to regain his stable.

China and I got into a heated conversation over the phone, and I told him I would see you on the track nigga! I was very ignorant to how the game works.

Once a whore decides to choose another pimp, you just lost an employee. Bottom line, your best choice is to get back down in the street and see if you can get her back.

Sasha and I would drive out to the bridge, and China was there waiting with his friends and some pistols.

As soon as Sasha had seen Candy, she jumps out of the car in her face and starts arguing. Candy was like a different person. We didn't even know who she was.

All the pimps would rush in to stop the situation from getting worse. An old school pimp broke the situation down.

He told me she could have gotten you killed over that whore whose right was to choose. It was a sweet tease of success in a beginners' lesson to the game.

With one dame, you can't rise to fame.

CHAPTER 13

THE MONEY TRAP

As I would take my daily fifteen minutes walks to Wonder Bread daily, I was back to being a square again

Candy had been gone for two months. My car had been repossessed. The credit card companies kept calling the house.

I realized I was living the money trap, in a slave to debt. I had nothing but only time to think about the mistakes I made and would never repeat. Pimping is a tuff process. However, I wanted to be different from the rest.

Years later, I learnt the true secrets to a pimp's success. I wanted to run it like a business with style and class. I started reading several different books as the time passed. Iceberg slim book "pimp," gave me the player's blueprint. Sasha had a true gift for the business. It was time to get back to the strip.

We started to understand what this game was all about. Sasha wanted to recruit other women to our bed and turn them out. This was our only option.

Playtime was now over. The game had only just begun. If we played this game, would our feelings stay the same?

The reality is this, you can't sell anything you love. However, look at the way the game was presented to us. After we decided to take our love to the other side. Our love for each other could be compromised.

All I could focus on was getting out of debt. My debt started to get out of hand. Creditors started garnishing my paycheck. I consulted a bankruptcy lawyer and filed over hundred thousand dollars in bankruptcy.

Now, I had all these fancy things to look at but no real assets. This is the one reason why poor people stay poor because they buy things with no value.

I vowed to myself, once I get out of this trap, I would never get caught up again. Wonder Bread would be my only strong source of income.

I made sure I was on time, and I tried to be a decent employee. I knew the industrial age was at its end and downsizing is profitable. I was one paycheck away from poverty. This could very well happen to anybody.

It was a working man's reality to believe in job security. All books that I started reading around that time broadcasted that the next big boom would be online.

This was 1997 and I knew nothing about computers. I knew we were leaving the industrial age and the information age was on its way in.

Even though we were in the money trap, maybe with the right idea, we could be in the money game. I rushed out and bought us a computer started an account with American online. They sent me a disk and now I felt like the world was at my fingertips.

I was totally amazed at the potential that you could promote any product or service for any business and reach massive amounts of people within a brief period from all over the world. This Internet was going to change the world in years to come.

Sasha would continue to perfect our sideline hustle. I would sell weed from time to time to help us make some extra money. Living in New York City was starting to become an expensive place to live.

My salary at Wonder Bread was just enough to make it. It was taking a while for us to produce any new whores.

All we really needed was a down ass bitch. Sasha told me she thought of a way to get Candy back from the strip.

Sasha said, she ran into an old boyfriend that she used to deal with and that he agreed if we paid him, he would pose as a trick and pick Candy up from the street.

Only thing, I would have to ride and get down in the back seat. Sasha and I had already got the word that China was back in jail.

She was with his bottom bitch in her wife in-laws. It was a perfect time to attack. We would both ride out there on a Friday night to the track. I got on the floor in the back seat, and we rolled around the streets.

I spotted her, he stopped, and she got in. I stayed on the floor until we drove off the strip then I got up. The bitch was in full shark!

When she saw me, I didn't hit her? I just told her, "Shut the fuck up, Sasha wants to talk to you." We broke some rules in the pimp game.

However, China posed as a trick to catch Candy in the beginning.

It was a move we made when he was weak. When I got Candy back to our apartment, Sasha convinced her because of her baby.

It was in her best interest to stay until her brother gets out of jail. Sasha would take her and work her from her friend Diane's house. Eventually, after six months, her brother Freaky came home from prison and she would return to him.

By that time, Candy story was up. Now, if Sasha would want to stay in this hustle, she would have to recruit her own girls and step up.

As a man, the woman that you have will reflect what type of man you are. At that time, Sasha inspired the greed that was inside me even if she was wrong or right. In pimping, it is believed, in order to be a great pimp, you must believe in your heart that all you're going to do is pimp.

The next four years we would run through massive amounts of women. Some would stay a while, and some would leave instantly.

The game was called cop in blow. And Brooklyn was our next show.

CHAPTER 14
WELCOME TO BROOKLYN

It was the year of 2000.

I was twenty-five years old, and Fredrick Junior was four years old. Our Mayor of New York city was Mayor Rudy Giuliani.

The President of our country was Bill Clinton and Carlos Slim was the richest man in the world.

Our most powerful company was General Motors and our nation's unemployment rate was at 3.9%. It was the start of a new era. We were at the end of the dotcom boom. Sasha and I decided we would move to Brooklyn in the summer of 2001.

Our one-bedroom was getting to be too expensive. It really killed me; I didn't want to move. I was born in Queens. My family and my life were a part of Queens. We decided to move to Herkimer Street in the Bedford- Stuyvesant area.

Sasha found a good deal for us out there. Brooklyn would take some time to get used to. Eventually, I ended up bidding for a job in Albany Avenue in Brooklyn, out of the bakery to one of Wonder Bread depots where we would pack the route trucks with their orders of bread, so they can deliver to grocery stores.

I ended up bidding for the head checkers position in Albany Avenue. There was one other guy named Larry I worked with on the job.

It was perfect for me. Larry and I worked by ourselves all night. The supervisor didn't come in until the last two hours of the day. Around Wonder Bread, it was a rumor that the supervisor at Albany Avenue was a real jerk.

It didn't matter though, I told myself how bad could it be? I wouldn't have to deal with him a whole shift.

When I started working there, Eddie was out because of his back. The supervisor filling in for Eddie told me Eddie would be back soon.

One week later, I would get to meet Eddie. I knew when I met him, I was going to have a problem.

I could remember when I started working at Albany Avenue. I took the bus every day from Herkimer Street in Brooklyn to Albany Avenue. Working in the depot was a lot of work. Every day finishing up, I was dead tired.

Sasha and I was whore less for a while. Now, it was like we were back to being a regular couple again. One beautiful fall morning, after getting home from work, I would never forget this day. After watching the news when I got home, Breaking news! Breaking news! The World Trade Center has been attacked.

All I did was watch the TV in disbelief.

Money making Manhattan in a place called New York city will never be forgotten. We would see people unite when needed in this time of crisis.

The New York police and fire department did an outstanding job. By the year ending, everything was okay with Albany Avenue.

I really missed Queens.

However, I was getting used to Brooklyn. By tax return time that year, I decided to buy a car so Sasha and I could get around a little better. I bought a 1994 Ford Taurus from the auto auction for about two thousand dollars.

No, it was not the greatest car.

Years later, I learnt cars are like whores. It is not about the looks, it's how dependable they are. Quoted by Master Pimp in the book called a Pimps Rap. Everything was coming together until one day at Albany Avenue, Larry and I was at the end of our shift, when Eddie the supervisor and Pedro his assistant came in.

Eddie kept complaining about my overtime. I mean, sometimes things cannot be helped. You may get a late truck that comes in and you try explaining to management.

Listen, I had about twenty route trucks to pack out and the product came in late. I had to stay a couple of hours.

Corporations will always try to do more with less. Overtime was becoming a big issue at Albany Avenue. Eddie would call me into the office that early morning.

Now, even though Larry and I had been drinking, I was in a pretty good mood. I do not know what came over me that day. I just flipped! Eddie asked me about the overtime. I tried to explain to him the situation.

We got into a very loud shouting match and Eddie sent me home for insubordination. That day, I got home. I contacted the union chairperson. He called me back that evening. He told me they were going to have a termination meeting on me.

Now, just like that, my job security was in jeopardy. I waited two weeks then we finally had the meeting at human resources where the bakery was located. That day, driving there, I am not going to lie, I was extremely nervous.

If I had been fired Sasha and I would have been in big trouble. Word around the bakery was, "I was gone." I was not the greatest employee and my record at Wonder Bread was not that good.

The meeting finally started, and Eddie stated that he felt threatened. They had to ask Pedro his assistant. I could not believe it, he said "no."

I silently said to myself, wow, I could not believe Pedro said no. I had won on a technicality. After that, Dean Crawford, the head of human resources told me he did not want to see me here again.

I was happy I did not get fired but deep down I was angry that this company could have that type of control over me; that at any time I could lose my job.

I hated the fact that a paycheck could define who I am.

It was like, I was a robot and someone else had the remote.

From that point on, I swore to myself; whatever I had to do to break the chains of corporate slavery, I would do it, even if I had to go out and pimp.

One day, visiting Sasha's mother, her cousin and I went to the weed spot to cop some green. As I pulled up and doubled parked outside of the spot, I sent Sasha's cousin in there.

Then out of nowhere, it was this ambulate truck, which could not avoid another car and made an unauthorized sharp turn in front of him.

The ambulate truck couldn't avoid hitting me! The driver of the ambulate truck, Ron Tackett got out and we exchanged information.

He said he was sorry, and he promised that his company would pay for the damages. I said OKAY, took his information and we left.

When I got back to Sasha's mother house, after telling Sasha about what happened, she urged me to go to the hospital. She said she would consult a lawyer immediately.

Sasha must have gotten the luck of the draw. She found some random lawyer. His name was Gary Wiess located in garden city in long Island.

Gary was an amazing accident lawyer. He managed everything over the phone. He told me to get to the hospital immediately because we needed an accident report.

I did everything that was asked and had an appointment set to take an m-r-I. I had to go to therapy five times a week.

When my m-r-I reports came back, the doctor told me I had three herniated discs in my lower back. After that, Gary contacted me and told me I had a case.

He also told me to get a cell phone, don't miss any therapy appointments. Now, I had a lawsuit, and I was out on disability from Wonder Bread.

It was time for Sasha and me to hit the street and recruit.

CHAPTER 15

FOR LOVE OR MONEY

For love or money, which one is more important in a relationship?

They say, for most relationships, the number one problem is finances. Could money make or break the love you feel for someone or does love really matter?

I was left with some hard choices to make between love or money.

The choices I would make would change my life forever. Now, with me out on disability from work, we had nothing but time to recruit.

I could remember Sasha and I decided to take a trip to South Carolina. We would let Aunt Kitten; Sasha's Aunt watch Fred junior at her mother's house in Queens.

He would also attend school over there where we felt at the time, that was the best place for Fred. We would go to South Carolina to see if we could recruit any girls in the town. Sasha's grandmother lived in Allendale South Carolina.

So, we drove down there, got a motel inside of town and then we went to see her grandmother.

We picked up one of her cousins and he took us to an area called flat street where all the local clubs were at, and everybody hung out.

I had brought a half of pound of weed with me.

My plan was to sell it while we were down there recruiting girls. Sasha and I would hang out on flat street to see if we could cop anything.

We noticed that all the girls were strung out on drugs, or they had a lot of babies. The next day, Sasha told me she wanted to drive into the woods to look for her cousins. We arrived there and the next day she ran into her cousin, Tam.

Tam was a young seventeen-year-old dark skin fine ass black girl that had a true look of a freak. A perfect cop for the New York City streets was before us.

Her living conditions were terrible. Her immediate family did not want anything to do with her. After Sasha and I witnessed this, we looked at each other with the same ambition. We knew she was a perfect cop; the only problem was her family.

Tam would beg us to come back with us the next day. We took her back with us to Brooklyn from that long ride back from South Carolina.

When we got back, it would be no time before her Aunty Betty would contact Sasha about Tam. Remember, now, nobody cared about this girl but as soon as we got her it was a problem. Sasha and I helped everybody out in both of our families, especially Aunty Betty. Do you think it mattered in the end?

Of course not. Sasha and Betty would get into an intense argument over the phone, and she threatened to call the police on us and tell them that we kidnapped Tam! I had to get on the phone with the chief of police and explain the situation to him.

I explain that she came up on her own will. I even had Tam get on the phone and explain to him that she was not kidnapped.

The law was, in South Carolina, after a girl turned seventeen years old, she is considered a woman. She has no more parental guidance. The chief of police told us, if that is what happened and he talked to Tam, then there is no charge.

Wow, what a relief. The family would be furious with us for years and I was told that I wasn't welcomed down there anymore which was okay with me and now it was time to get down to business.

I remember one day in Queens, walking down Jamaica avenue, I ran into Candy. We hugged each other and then she came and sat with me, and we just talked. I knew I could cop Candy.

I could remember she always had a crush on me. It was time for me to use that to my advantage. It would be the only way I could persuade her my way.

The reality was, Sasha was not really pimping hard on Candy. I knew this could be an easy cop. I gave Candy my number and told her she can choose me any time she wanted. Sasha's brother, Freaky was locked up again, so she was left out there by herself.

I could tell that Candy was a real veteran now and from the looks of her, the streets had beaten her down. Candy would be a great pull for us right now being that we just copped Tam. She had to learn the blueprint of the pimp game, how the pimps and whores worked and how the cops worked.

Who would be better than Candy to teach Tam the rules of the New York City jungle of prostitution? After a couple of days, Candy calls. I picked her up and dropped her off to her new family. It was a Friday night.

All of us were in our Brooklyn apartment and Sasha was getting them ready for the track. I avoided taking them out to Queen's bridge.

I wanted to try something new. I took them both down to twenty-eight street in Lexington in money-making Manhattan.

The first night was a disaster. I could not get them both on the same page. This track was too fast for them. After getting them back to the apartment that night in Brooklyn, I gave both of those bitches a tongue lashing.

I told them if they could not find a way to work together, then get the fuck out my face. Pimping is tuff, it is always a test. A whore will always test you to see how serious you are about your money.

As a pimp, you can't be weak. You must be able

to show extreme leadership in order to get paid. The next night, I took them to a slower track. It was time to see if I was cut out to be a pimp.

I got both of those bitches up at 3am in the morning and took them to the legendary Hunts Point track in the Bronx.

This night was a little better. Tam had a lot of complaints for a new whore. The next couple weeks that went by between both, Sasha and I was getting about five hundred dollars a night.

Things were coming together. GEICO insurance company sent me a check for six-thousand dollars lost wages. Being that I was going to be hustling these New York city streets, I bought a money green 1995 Dodge stratus.

A perfect hustle car to get around New York city. I noticed that Candy was starting to get jealous of Tam. Tam who was better looking was starting to grab more attention than the veteran Candy and being that I was not touching them it created more of a problem. I knew eventually, Candy would blow.

Two weeks later, Candy skipped off with some guy from Brooklyn, just leaving Tam. I told her she would have to pick up the slack from Candy.

She did and Tam in the next couple of weeks was bringing in five hundred dollars a night. Tam was very attracted to me, and I knew eventually, she would want me to service her. In my heart I needed a whore, and I would do whatever I had to do to keep Tam paying me. I was turned out!

I told her I would fuck her when she turned eighteen. I had to play mind games with her, or I think I would have lost her quicker than I did. Tam and I formed a good understanding. I turned her out myself.

I watched over Tam every night as she would walk the streets in those erotic revealing outfits and turn trick after trick.

She became a dam good whore. The cars would be lined up waiting for this sexy chocolate young hooker.

It was about eight months we had her we had already broke Pam for thousands of dollars. I could remember the first time I serviced Tam. It was on a Sunday.

It was kind of slow on the track that night, so I took Tam to the Executive Inn off the Whitestone expressway. All the pimps and tricks used this motel.

When we pulled up, Tam had a big smile on her face like she was so glad the wait was over. When we got in the room, she sat on the bed with her sexy chocolate body looking so seductive watching me as I rolled us some weed.

I am not going to lie. After watching her for months, I could not wait to get my hands on her young chocolate body. I told her to come and sit on my lap.

I took my hands and felt all over her young soft body aggressively. Sticking my tongue in her mouth and kissing her very seductively.

Whispering in her ear, "you are with your pimp now and you are my whore, don't be nervous."

My job was to make her feel secure while taking full control of her mind, body, and soul. Making her young wet pussy tingle with pleasure, she would ask to taste my treasure. I said, "yes" and she grabbed my Johnson, took her young wet sexy lips and started to pleasure me with the deep strokes of her mouth!

Not wanting to hit my high note too fast, I would stop her and turned her over and open those thick dark legs to taste her sweet young chocolate pussy listening to her moan with deep pleasure.

I would take my Johnson and push into her young wet trap; Tam would bring me to a very satisfying climax.

I also knew that she would want me to service her again in the near future. Tam didn't know what to expect that night.

When you have a prostitute, you must be unpredictable and spontaneous.

Whatever games you are selling the whore, she must sell it to the trick. This is the reverse side of pimping.

Only master pimps know how to play this game on its highest level. Working the tracks in New York city up late nights, chasing the essence of the game and the street life, it all had me hooked!

There was no better feeling. I was a true hustler from the streets. Between Hunts point and

Queensbridge, I was moving around the New York City jungle of prostitution and at that point, that became the solution.

We were finally on the fast track. I had really learned how to turn a woman out. That being squared, I love you gospel did not matter anymore. After learning the pimp game, I learned that you must throw away whatever you believed as a kid about women.

Whatever you were taught about living happily ever after marriage; that whole traditional relationship dream that you have or been sold or taught no longer exist.

A true pimp is only a reflection of his whores that he sends to work every night, while a square loves to trick with them.

A pimp's greatest asset is knowing what to say or when to touch a whore. A pimp is really a prostitute that must be able to sell himself or herself all the time.

Love to me now was just a mirage. However, my money trap was now solved.

CHAPTER 16
A PIMP'S AFFAIR

The cold-blooded reality in the pimp game is a pimp is a lonely person who really lives a lonely life.

He can only depend on and always trust himself. My relationship with Sasha should have been over the minute I knew I wanted to become a pimp.

Pimping in love don't mix. You can't profit off anything that you love. What I did with Tam that night would change Sasha and our relationship forever. I would look her in her face knowing in my heart I was deceiving her.

I was really defying my friend at times and things from that point on would only get worse. Tam's story would start to end sooner than I thought.

Tam started getting arrested a lot in Queen's bridge with Sasha, I knew it was a matter of time before she blew. Master pimps know and understand that the whole key to having any prostitute is mental psychology.

I violated some rules between Sasha and I. Tam

wanted Sasha's position and I knew that. Tam would get out of jail one last time.

However, this time, she had no plans to return. I tried to set her up with a trick. I knew she was dating. I told the trick to meet her at a McDonalds that I knew in Queens. When she had seen me, she must have thought I was going to whip her ass!

As soon as we stepped outside, she ran! Tam was quick, she was gone. I was caught in a twisted trap with Tam. With my greedy intentions, it was just to service her that night. The longer you can get a whore to stay, the longer she pays.

It was Sasha's cousin, one of us had to touch her. I decided to go back to work it had been. About eight months, we had saved up a ten-thousand-dollar bankroll off Tam with the lawsuit in play.

Sasha was still recruiting; I knew it wouldn't be long before we were back in business.

Not knowing what you need to know when you supposed to know it, can hurt you. Timing is everything in life and business.

It wasn't long before Sasha started talking to this other young stripper from Florida named Rita. Rita was a young nineteen-year-old Black slim sexy freaky bisexual female that was messing with some stud from Florida.

Sasha told me that she was going to fly her in from Florida. This wouldn't be the last time we would fly in different turnouts.

I could remember picking Rita up from the airport. The minute I picked her up, by just looking at her, I got a feeling that this was a winner.

Sasha was a decent recruiter. She got into the car, we made small talk and I can tell by the way she was looking at me, she was very attracted. On the way driving back home, my only hopes were that Sasha and Rita hit it off. For everything to work I needed Sasha to be a complete freak!

What I just went through with Tam, I didn't want to happen this time. We finally got to Brooklyn. I took her upstairs and introduced Sasha to Rita. They seemed like they were cool. Later that night, I had to go to work.

So, it was a perfect night for them to hit it off. I left later that evening to go to work. When I got back the next day, Sasha said they just chilled for the whole night.

From the impression I got, I knew they really didn't hit it off that good. I knew it was a situation I couldn't rush.

However, Rita was hot for me. That day, I just chilled out and watched Rita and Sasha play with each other. As we would all smoke weed and listen to music.

It was Rita's turn out night for the track. She had never walked the track before. I took her to Hunts Point the first night.

Rita really did not need Sasha's assistance fixing herself up. For a young broad, she was very independent.

She was a perfect turn out for a pimp who was whoreless or on the bottom.

Before putting her down, I needed to get the real rundown on this young fresh turnout. Rita and I rolled some weed up and before going to the track we just talked.

She told me her father was a correction officer that worked for Rikers island. Her mother lived in Virginia and her mother and father was divorced because the father turned gay. Rita also had a little small son from an older man she was with.

Rita's mother left her a two-bedroom condominium not too far from where we lived on Herkimer Street. Her mother told her for five hundred dollars a month the condominium was hers. I knew from after getting the lowdown from her, there was a good chance I could make some money with her. She was in a desperate situation and in need of money.

The first night with Rita was business as usual. I would turn her out myself just like I did Tam. Just like Tam, I would watch Rita all night turn trick after trick. Rita was a natural whore and a natural for the game.

After a couple of weeks with Rita, I use to send her out there with no panties. When she wore those short revealing skirts, every time she bent over in a trick's car, tricks would drive up from nowhere to be next!

After a while, all the pimps were trying to knock me for the bitch! Just like when I had Tam. With my bad luck though, Sasha and Rita weren't hitting it off. I knew sooner or later with the money she was bringing; she was craving for someone to hold her and caress her mind, body and soul. Rita and I hit it off pretty good in the streets.

We had a pretty good chemistry. On the weekends She could bring in a thousand dollars in one night. I could remember the first time I touched Rita.

She went on a hotel date at the Executive Inn. This was the same motel I turned Tam out.

I don't know what turned me on more than the fact that she just broke a trick for the money she was about to give me, or the fact that I knew I had a real whore on my hands. After ten minutes Rita came back in the room.

She threw the money on the dresser and the sexual attraction between us was unbelievable! Rita with her slutty-sexy ways, aggressively took my Johnson out and started to suck me off like she owned my dick than she rode me like a jockey in the Kentucky Derby! This bitch was a true freak.

The whore's money was right, her pussy was tight. I would remember this whore for life. Now, my biggest problem was getting Sasha and Rita on the same page.

There was one night when I was talking to Rita on the phone and Sasha beeps in, I thought I had clicked Sasha off when I put her on hold to talk back to Rita. She heard the whole conversation. She knew all about our affair.

When I got back, Sasha drilled me all night

until finally I just came clean and told her everything. She replies to me how could you do that behind my back! I told her how I could come to you and tell you what I have done!

I begged her just to go along with it. This is what the game is about. I knew Rita wanted to be with me and wanted Sasha out of the picture. What was I supposed to do? Who did my loyalty lie with? Deep down it was with Sasha. Rita was the one bringing in the money and was Sasha's recruit.

Sasha called Rita on the phone and Rita chose me on the phone. Sasha accuses me of stealing Rita from her! Was she serious? I didn't have to still her Rita wanted me from the beginning.

If I truly wanted to, I could have done anything I wanted with Rita. The situation would only grow worse if I could describe her rage in words.

The house looked like a hurricane hit it! She stormed out the house going to confront Rita! I always knew in my heart the square part of our relationship would have to be broken and this might have been the only way we could leave the square part of us in the past.

I was already turned out; it was no turning back.

By the time I got to Rita, Sasha was already up there with Rita trying to convince her to leave me and choose her.

It was the first time I saw her so angry because she was hurt. Sasha, out of complete anger stormed out the apartment.

I just let her go outside. I stayed upstairs in Rita's apartment trying to just figure things out. By the time I got downstairs, my car looked like it came out of the junk yard! I had only myself to blame for this nonsense.

Sasha ended up leaving and taking the stash of fourteen hundred dollars I had saved up from Rita. Rita told me don't worry about it, will make more daddy. My money, my apartment, everything, is yours.

What was I supposed to do? Every pimp I knew would have stepped off with the bitch that was paying them, offering them a brand-new pad so I can lay up with her. I knew in my heart I had Rita.

All I had to do was leave Sasha and tell Rita it's going to be just her. I wanted to, so bad and I told Rita "Yeah, ok, just until I can figure things out!"

After a couple of days away from Sasha, I started to feel bad about how things went down especially after Fred Junior called me.

My last option was to toss her up to another pimp.

That means my career as a pimp would be in jeopardy. The word on the tracks would be why would he toss up a young fresh whore? Where is his pimping? He isn't no real pimp because a real pimp doesn't toss any fresh young whore unless she's a problem.

I needed time to figure things out. I didn't want to blow Sasha. My guilt for Sasha would make me unwillingly toss her up to a pimp I met from Hunts

Point. His name was Rock. Rock was in the same position as I was.

He had one whore on the street looking to cop his next bitch. Through previous conversations with Rita, I knew she had a crush on his bottom bitch.

Rita stayed with Rock about a month. She called me back after a month and asked me to come back. This time it wasn't the same, the game I ran on her became lame.

After she came back, I didn't pimp on her like I did the first time. I barely went on the track with her. I blew her after two weeks and that was it. This pimp's affair would turn into a nightmare. I had a lot of soul-searching to do.

My relationship with my son wasn't the greatest. I was in the streets all the time. I never saw him. I didn't even know how to be a father.

My job was always in jeopardy. The reality was this was a square relationship. If things were ever going to work, we would have to be completely honest with each other about everything.

Even if she decided she wanted to be a whore, I was ready to accept that. I knew in my heart it wouldn't be an easy transition.

However, my chips were all in at this point. Time in time again I would beat myself up about staying with Sasha.

I knew in my heart it was over. I couldn't be a cold-blooded pimp and push my kid's mother out. Love in this business cannot exist.

I knew one thing at that point; if I didn't know anything else, I was lost and turned out.

CHAPTER 17

THE MONEY GAME

The year was now 2004.

Our Mayor of New York city was billionaire Michael Bloomberg. He won an historical three terms in Gracie mansion.

The President of the United States was George W. Bush. The Richest person in the world was still Microsoft founder, Bill Gates and our most powerful company was Walmart. Our country's unemployment rate was at 5.4%.

What is the money game? Who are the players and what are the rules of the game? All through my life I wanted to understand the money game.

What is the difference between being rich or wealthy? Is there an actual difference? They say that top one percent controls most of the wealth.

What is the cold-blooded blueprint to the economic ladder to success? Is it just controlled by a chosen few? Or does this American dream exist for everyone? The true gospel is, we are all a slave to money in one way or another, rich or poor.

Can money be all our universal religion and some of us just don't know it? I decided at one point I would take my shot at becoming a participant in the money game on December 10, 2004.

This was four days before my twenty-ninth birthday.

Sasha and I would start www.bestkeptsecrets69.com with a hundred and fifty thousand dollars inheritance from her grandmother, on her father's side of the family split three ways between Sasha and her two brothers.

This happen a month after Rita had split and one year later, September 2004, I settled a seventy-five thousand dollars lawsuit.

After lawyer fees, I walked away with forty-eight thousand dollars.

Between Sasha and I, we had over ninety thousand dollars. I told myself this is a once in a lifetime opportunity.

A shot to take this money, flip it, and gain full financial security. If we could produce the right plan for our money, we decided to take the ultimate shot at our own company which would make us players in the money game.

Sasha had produced the idea of a dating site, where people could link up all over and meet each other. Now, I'll be honest, I didn't think it was a bad idea.

However, I didn't want to do it! Sasha and I knew nothing about building a website. We were rolling the dice if we decided to continue with this idea.

We would be learning everything as we went along. When starting a new company, you must have the right execution plan, the start-up costs, how many members you will need on your team, what is the mission of the company.

All my life, I wanted to run my own company. I decided I'm going to do it whether it works. However, I knew I was gambling. I felt deep down, this could be my way out of corporate slavery. And out, to avoid the streets and jail with the tears of inspiration dropping from my eyes.

And the heart of a lion from the deep jungle, there is no feeling like the hunt for success. Sasha and I decided to call it www.bestkeptsecrets69.com LLC.

There, we were participants in the money game. With the fees, we set up the corporation in building the website. Our total cost was about five thousand dollars.

Sasha and I had been out of the game for a while. We were back to being a regular couple again. Considering everything that happened; however, it wouldn't last long.

I decided to bid back in the sanitation department at Wonder Bread in Jamaica Queens where I started.

I had about nine years in Wonder Bread and did not accomplish anything working there. I was just able to survive and pay bills.

Was my true reality a scary one? Was I going to

end up like some old gees do, with a bunch of war stories as you would hear and see most of the old gees in the streets, who was rich and then poor? Or was I going to be part of the chosen few who took their money and turn it into something big?

Did you ever hear the quote from the movie "The Mack?" (Being rich in black means something) or does it matter? After starting Bestkeptsecrets, our landlord was going to sell the house. I started looking at some houses to purchase.

However, real estate was at an all-time high. We held off on purchasing a home. We decided to look at some houses across the water.

By January 2005, everything was in play. The company was set up and we had launched the website. We proceeded to purchase the company's trademark.

With the rumors around the bakery, that the bakery in Philadelphia might replace Jamaica, I knew sooner, or later Wonder Bread would be a memory.

With Bestkeptsecrets being a new start-up company, I knew it could be years before we could make any money.

It was time to hit the streets again. This time, we were playing for high stakes. I felt that with all our experience and everything we had been through.

Let's face it. We were together since the room on Southgate Street. Sasha stayed with me through all the tuff times.

I was so willing to bet on us.

By the spring of 2005, we had finally moved to New Jersey. I knew this guy I worked with and met in the early years of Wonder Bread. His name was Warren.

We were both jobbers when we met on the shipping dock. Warren was an old hustler from Hollis Queens who did a little time in jail and started working at Wonder Bread looking for a fresh start, trying to avoid the streets.

Years later, Warren started working for a real estate company called Affordable Homes. I tried to work with someone I knew personally and give a fellow associate some business.

One of the rules in business; avoid doing business with so-called friends who you think just because you are giving them your business, they have your best interests in mind. In business, we must investigate everybody you do business with.

Friends or company or any type of investments, it doesn't matter. Scammers come in all forms. Warren showed me some places in New Jersey, Newark Irvington area. I mean, where else could he have shown me.

He was new to the business. However, timing is everything. He got in at the right time. It was the middle of a real estate boom.

Sasha and I decided to take a place in Irvington New Jersey. We met with Warren, we gave him the money and across the water, here we come!

After two weeks of finally moving in, everything hit us like an atomic bomb. I found out, Affordable Homes were being investigated for fraud and the owners were being indicted. The courts froze all Affordable Homes assets.

This situation had created a lot of instability with Sasha and me. We knew we had to move with a sense of urgency. We knew we had a little time.

However, we just didn't know how much time we had.

Everybody that had rented apartments from Affordable Homes was able to stay there rent-free until the whole situation was solved.

To make matters worse, we were living in an extremely high crime area. I knew it was a pretty tuff area, but the gang violence was ridiculous.

How was I going to build my new company under all these crazy circumstances? We were already basically all in.

We had no choice!

The money we had, started to dwindle away. I needed Wonder Breads income, even though there were rumors of Jamaica bakery closing.

Warren took our money knowing the situation Affordable Homes were in. He also rented me that house in that high crime area knowing how bad it was.

He had green eyes. He had changed after working with those Jews who owned Affordable Homes. I just thought as a friend he could have hipped me to some better places that he was renting in Jersey.

Sasha and I decided to get back in the business. She started recruiting again; she never stopped. We were in a different state, a new place, a lot to figure out.

Most of all, it was time to build Bestkeptsecrets and deal with whatever problems that came our way. Warren ended up refunding our security deposit and first month's rent. Things between Warren and I would never be the same… the money game.

Will it make me or break me? I don't know. The road to success could sometimes be a bumpy road. However, it's a much-needed ride.

I can only learn from my mistakes. Even though that ride might sometimes be a lonely one.

CHAPTER 18

SASHA'S WHITE PAY DAY

Prostitution! What is the reality about prostitution?

Is it morally wrong for a woman to sell her services for money? Or is it just a business like every other business?

After my time on the track for years understanding the prostitution business entirely. I learned when it came to women, it was about money and choice. If it was the track or escort service, women make a choice to sell their services.

The reality is, there were professional ladies of leisure before pimps. Another reality is, there will be women of leisure after pimps.

Especially in this greedy capitalist society we live in. At this point, Sasha and I had started a dating site.

We were already in the business of bringing people together in some way or another. The temptation, the greed factor, the easy money-making drive, was not enough to lead me back in the world that changed my life.

The coldblooded desire in my heart to see our company get built as soon as possible, finally gave me a shot to beat job security in take control of my own soul. This would lead me back to the gritty streets.

I was ready to win my chips was all in. This time, I said to myself, I would do things differently. The street game for pimping was starting to become ancient. It wasn't about the streets anymore; it was now about the rise of the internet.

A new game would arrive—this was online prostitution. Sites like craigslist and back page made it possible for any woman to sell her services.

This business is taking a paradigm shift. Prostitution is now adopting a digital approach, and this was going to be the new order in a few years.

I and Sasha had to level up to the game.

Without having a pimp, more women would be renegading. However, the game never changes, just the players. It was time for us to adapt.

We decided to start an escort service, which was an underground division for the company. I was hoping we could create revenue until the site would start to generate income.

I saw how other ethnic groups operated their business when it came to prostitution. It was usually all business. The girls made salaries; they didn't operate like your traditional Black pimps. I wasn't in it for the Bragg or the flash, I was just in it for the cash.

For me to fully learn the escort business, I got a job as a driver and started working with different agencies all around New York City.

I needed to gain some experience and I loved it. I would collaborate with different women and make contacts with other call girls that were in the business. Just like I had learned the pimp game, I learned everything about the escort business. Sasha would meet a young girl that would come in and change our life forever.

Her name was Mandy. She was an Irish girl from Allentown, Pennsylvania. I could remember the first time I met Mandy and her friend, Sarah.

They were young recruits who were brought in to help build our new startup company. I picked them both up at the legendary forty-second street at the port authority in money-making Manhattan.

I drop them both off at a hotel. Sasha had got for that night. The funny thing is, I didn't like Mandy. I felt that she would be the one to put the finishing touches on the little relationship we had left.

This was Sasha's turn out and first real lesbian experience. In the back of my mind, I said at one point, she would be our demise.

Sasha had an old friend; her name was Diane. She would use her apartment from time to time to meet females and she started meeting with Mandy secretly. That's when I knew deep down, I would eventually end up losing Sasha.

It was just a matter of time. I started thinking that it was time for me to get the raw reality of being a pimp. I needed someone who was on top to give me a better understanding of the world of prostitution.

It was time to reach out to a master player. So, I would go to Queens, to the first place I rented to see my old landlord, the legend, Allan Robinson. At this point in my life, all my relationships we're in jeopardy.

My father and I never spoke; I couldn't talk to him. My mother and Joe Brooks had gotten married; that was devastating for my father. My mother and I kept a decent relationship. I barely ever saw, my son.

At Wonder Bread, my job was always in jeopardy. My life had become extremely complicated. It was time for me to look at the raw reality of how things were. I felt in a lot of ways I had sold myself to the world of the unknown.

I was a true risk-taker at heart. I kept telling myself, there is no room for mistakes or failure. The more you know, the harder it gets.

However, I wasn't going to quit. I decided to go see Al in Queens. He was this type of man; either you loved him because you understood him or hated him.

It was no in-between. I needed some advice from someone who played the game at the very top. I knew many pimps though.

Al was the only one I felt I could come to, and Al

use to love cognac.

I stopped by the liquor store and bought a bottle of Hennessy to give him. When I arrived there, Al was right there sitting in his front living room, like he was on the lookout.

I told him I wanted to talk to him about some things concerning the business. With his deep voice, he told me to sit down. I handed over the bottle of Hennessy and he said to me, "yes, this is Kool! Fred this will mix well with cocaine."

Al takes the coke out and takes a hit. Then passes it to me.

I had a virgin nose when it came to snorting girl. I took a hit and dam, I felt like the world was just lifted off my shoulders.

All the pressure I was feeling had just taken a brief getaway. He asked me why I was there. He said again to me, wait a second let me tell you, why you are here?

You are in search for information, and you can't relate to anybody in your age group. Am I about, right? I replied, yes! I told him I came to you because I know you know this business and what it takes to be a pimp.

Al told me; you dam right, I do. I had over a hundred toes on concrete! As he would take a deep snort of that lady, he would get extremely arrogant. He would brag about his days of being on top of the game.

Obviously, Al had all the information I needed. I had to sit and listen to the old gee give me the rundown like I was a clown auditioning for an act in the circus, Al was a real character. When I got ready to split, I was so high from the cocaine mix with the weed I smoked. I felt like I was sent up to space.

Subsequently, I made sure I went over there every day so I can soak his brain for the right game I needed.

Al wasn't in the greatest position. The judge had frozen all his assets which he had owned a considerable number of buildings in Brooklyn.

He had lost almost everything he had.

Al loved cars but he didn't even have a car to get around.

When you look up the word corruption, you would see Al's name in the dictionary. I never met a more corrupted soul than his.

He could corrupt a baby if he had to. He was a real cold-blooded animal from the jungle. Al and I would hang out together every night.

We stayed up late sniffing cocaine and drinking Cognac. Al started to respect me. He would ask me if I could come over and take him to see his mother from time to time. She was in the hospital fighting for her life at the old age of eighty.

Al told me, "I'm going to take you to Manhattan." Al showed me the top of both worlds, the black side, and the white side.

First, he took me to Harlem, to the famous Seville. It was a bar owned by his uncle in moneymaking Manhattan.

GAMBLING PROSTITUTION AND DRUGS

All the prostitute pimps' con men hung out there. Always, his uncle would have his all-green custom-made Cadillac Seville parked in front of the bar.

Al was a true star in Harlem. He would also take me to a famous strip club located in Manhattan. Al knew the owner who was an Italian guy.

They had known each other for years. He would take Al and I to a restaurant on the east side where we would sit in the back and sniff cocaine. I could remember this man asking me, "do you know what Al and I are talking about?"

He was as serious as a mother fucker. He spooked me! I said, "no, I don't." Al would say to me, "you, see? You got what you ask for." I said, "what is that?" He said, "what the fuck you think Fred? Corruption… mother fucker!"

I felt like I was in a movie.

Over there, Sasha had been busy spending a lot of time with Mandy.

I started spending a lot of time to myself and lady cocaine became my new woman. Al became my new best friend. I knew at some point I was going to have to decide about Wonder Bread. Everything was happening so fast.

I really didn't know where I was going to end up. Sasha and I would finally move Mandy in with us. Sasha's white payday was either going to be a big pay off or a big rip-off; only time could tell.

I could only hope that at one point, everything would come together eventually. I knew in my heart; I was getting ready to go through the biggest transition in my life.

I was nervous that I would learn the true reality of what I have been chasing.

This transition would not be an easy one.

CHAPTER 19
CATCHING THE BIG FISH

As I write this book, it makes me think about all the mistakes I made in my life.

I was my worst enemy at times. I could remember counting my last ten thousand dollars saying to myself, wow it's almost gone!

It had been two years since we had come into about ninety thousand dollars between the two of us. Reality is money can be your best friend or your worst enemy; depending on how you treat it.

A day after celebrating Sasha's Birthday in late June, the year 2006, the next day at Wonder Bread I fell fifteen feet on a faulty ladder!

It was one of the most horrific times in my life. I was awarded on the job compensation and that was it for Wonder Bread.

The money had to come from somewhere until Sasha decided to turn Mandy out. It was time for Mandy to earn her keep. She had lived for free off us for too long. After the cocaine, I had given her in all the wild nights with Sasha.

Mandy got used to the easy lifestyle. It was time for her to put up or shut up. I knew she was hot for

Sasha's hot sexy seductive ways. There were times I would walk in and watch Mandy riding Sasha's hot pussy.

Until she exploded with excitement all over Sasha's wet trap. I would watch them from time to time with deep lust and curiosity.

I knew after secretly watching them those late erotic nights, Sasha really enjoyed being with other women.

Could I have lost her, or did the game flip on me?

Sasha was my only gateway to get paid off this white bitch who we needed desperately to get out there and turn extra revenue for the company. I could remember Mandy's turnout was a tuff one.

Most of the time, it is when you are turning from a square to a freak. Most women will never admit it. But there is a whore inside every woman. It's their inner personality. All it comes down to is, will they bring the other side out?

After the big struggle with Sasha, Mandy decided she would do it. I remember her first date, Sasha would fix her up to be a real sexy looking young white call girl.

It was my job to teach her the streets and how the business worked and protect Bestkeptsecrets' new poster girl.

Mandy would work the phones and post her pictures on the websites. It was my job to drive her to her calls. This was not the track anymore; it was our escort service. I could remember taking her on her very first date.

The date was set for four hundred dollars an hour. She had a nervous face. On the way driving there, I broke down the blueprint of a call girl's hustle to her. I told her what to look out for, what to expect and never to worry about anything because I'll always be right outside.

I instructed her, call me when you collect the money because that's when the hour starts and when the hour ends, I will call you on the phone.

Either he pays again for the next hour or the date's over. I told her, whenever I called, pick up quickly. She started to understand how to run the friend and companionship game on tricks where she didn't have sex at all or would make them pay extra for her services.

She learned how to sell dreams of fantasy, not sex. That is a good call girl's best asset.

Mandy was hooked to the fast money lane and the raw cocaine. Al had shown me where to get it from in Harlem. She got use to the easy life of having no bosses.

Within a month, she was getting four hundred dollars an hour from dates with no problems.

Until one early morning, we got a call from Morris town, New Jersey. I was well rested that morning; however, a true hustler must be ready to go.

The call was for four hundred dollars an hour at the Grove manor hotel in Morris town. I took the call. At that point, we were just starting to get on our feet, and we needed money. The call came about three o' clock in the morning. It was my first time driving to different counties in New Jersey.

To this day, always, I faulted myself for letting greed override me from not seeing all the angles because that bust could have been avoided.

Why didn't I pay attention to that fucking police car that was parked in the hotel parking lot that early morning? In my mind, I am just a cab.

However, the cops wanted blood that night. I started slipping and I examine the situation wrong. I let her out the car in front of that parked police car. Which I had learned later that it was just bad timing for me. They were there to investigate a stolen car ring.

They saw me let this young white female out the car at that time of the morning. They knew what she was going in the hotel for, and they followed her up to the room. The John that ordered her, they threatened to call his wife.

He told them right away he found her on a website, and we were done!

I called Mandy immediately after I examine the situation, and told her to leave the hotel, the cops are coming! To this day, I do not know why she didn't get out of the hotel fast enough.

I called Sasha and told her there is a possibility I'm going to jail.

By that time, the police were already there telling me to get out the car. They asked me what was I doing? I told them I'm a cab, I just dropped some one-off. They didn't buy that.

They brought Mandy and the trick out. They arrested me for promoting prostitution and arrested Mandy for the solicitation of prostitution.

To this day, I don't know what they did with the trick because I didn't see him come with us to the police station.

On the way there, I looked at Mandy's face and it was her first time getting arrested. I knew she was scared!

When we arrived at the police station, they separated us. The way Mandy looked, with very young features as if she was underage. However, I knew she was eighteen years old. All they had on me was a promoting prostitution charge.

They drilled both of us.

Mandy followed the plan. She kept her mouth shut! The cop called the judge at that time in the morning and my bail would be set at five thousand dollars with ten percent down. I knew we barely had any money.

I think I had a hundred dollars in my pocket in which I had wished I had left home. I wanted to try to get Mandy out first.

They towed my car away with high towing fees per day. I was in there about a week until my oldest sister Roxanne had driven Sasha up there. My mother had to lend me the money to get out. When I got out, I had a case.

I had to go to Morris town until the case was over. We got Mandy out and then it was back to business as usual. I ended up pleading guilty to promoting prostitution.

The judge gave me a year probation and community service and of course, I had to pay a fine.

AL had come to New Jersey to see me when I got out. Sasha told me while I was in there, he tried to cop her and Mandy. In this business, you can't trust anyone; not even people you think is your friends in your time of need.

They will try to take full advantage of you. I knew from that point; I couldn't trust him. As time went on, Mandy was now making thousands of dollars!

Her biggest catch would come when she caught a big fish. His name was Jack, and he was the ex-Mayor of a town in New Jersey. It was time to play long con.

I told Mandy to tell him she was a young college girl, who has a roommate and that she is trying to finish college. The fish went for it. His dates would start at eight hundred dollars for two hours until paying her thousands to stay overnight.

Jack paid upfront and she would bring the money right to the car when I dropped her off. It was a sensational feeling, breaking a trick for that type of money.

I had a loud laugh in the car all the way back to Irvington after collecting the money.

Things for a while started to come together. I saw a big change in Sasha and Mandy. They would start to argue a lot.

It seems that Mandy's rise to fame started to affect her brain. This happens to most whores who start making that type of money and tricks start going nuts over them. This situation would only become worst in time to come!

Sasha's white payday was giving us a big headache. It was extremely hard to build a stable around her.

Mandy couldn't accept being the bottom bitch. Some other recruits Sasha had brought in, she didn't want anyone else getting close to her.

She blew them all! I knew deep down; an escort service cannot run on one girl.

In time to come, if Mandy leaves Sasha, and I would hit the bottom in no time.

CHAPTER 20

NOTHING LAST FOREVER

While the year of 2006 would be a year to remember, the year 2007 would be one of the worse years in my life.

Now, it was early 2008.

Everything that could go wrong went wrong that year. I mean, I lost everything! I was totally brought to my knees!

By December 14, 2007, Wonder Bread and I decided to part ways. After twelve years, the act was finally over. Sasha decided to leave me. She blamed me for everything that went wrong. As much as it hurt me losing her, I had to let go.

Sasha was truly everything to me.

However, we choose a life where love don't exist. Mandy had left late 2006. She had to go see her parents one more time for Thanksgiving.

When she came back, she wasn't the same. When she went back to see her parents for Christmas, Mandy would never return.

She blew a ten-thousand-dollar date with Jack. Mandy tried to control Sasha with the money she was making. I left them two alone a lot staying to take care of business. Mandy and Sasha's relationship became complicated. It had been months since Sasha, and I was intimate. In some ways we became strangers just business partners.

I could remember going to see Al in his new Mini mansion in St Alban's. He told me, "I'm going to give it to you as raw as this cocaine.

The bitch is not yours. She's Sasha's!" He said, "you have no control over the situation. Yeah, you might have set up the escort service, but Sasha controls the bitch, not you."

He said all of this to me after I dropped Sasha and Mandy to Pennsylvania. He spoked the true gospel to me.

There was nothing I could say or really do. I could only sit there with that straw up my nose in think about what he just laid on me.

He told me this, months before the bitch split. Months later, after she left and I told him she left, he said, "man, you just went through a crazy set of circumstances and your financial freedom is gone."

At the time when he told me this, I didn't know how bad of an impact its months would be to come. Sasha couldn't hide depression.

She tried to play it off at first. I guess in her mind, she thought she would come back. Sasha recruited another female named Hollywood.

We had put her on a thousand-dollar date with Jack. Meanwhile, Sasha went to Allentown to try to bring Mandy back.

Hollywood was a fine freaky Latino female from the Bronx. She was more into women. Sasha and Hollywood couldn't find the right rhythm. She blew her quickly. After Mandy left, I knew we would be up against the ropes.

Mandy had built a minimum four hundred dollars an hour client list, including our most lucrative client, Jack. How do you replace that overnight? We had a couple of girls on call part time from some of my contacts I made.

When I was a driver at other escort services. Mandy was our main best girl. She was the site administrator and responsible for the daily operations of the site. How could I let the whole company depend on one girl?

This was my worst mistake.

When she left, everything crumbled one by one. The rest of the year, I tried to fight to hold things together. Sasha asked me to drive down to Pennsylvania so she can try to bring her back. Mandy wouldn't even answer the door.

We stayed at a local hotel, and we left in the morning with no Mandy. One day, Mandy came in desperate need of money to do a two-thousand-dollar date with Jack.

I dropped Sasha and Mandy back to Allentown so they could have time with each other. I knew the game. Mandy needed attention but at this point it didn't matter. I was trying to save the company, I had to.

I was ready to do anything to keep the money

flowing. We desperately needed her at that point. Sasha couldn't bring her back to live with us because Mandy's parents got in her head.

At this point, Wonder Bread income was my only option and my time at Wonder Bread was coming to an end. I had overslept and got a no call, no show.

My record was very bad. I went back out on disability from work trying to buy time. While I was out of Wonder Bread, I got back into the wholesale business, selling hats and t-shirts, to bring in extra money.

I set up a table in a car wash in Irvington where the owner let me stay there rent-free. The union representative called me and told me when I come back, they were going to have a termination meeting on me.

I said Okay. I called Ben Blaze, the supervisor and told him to set up the meeting.

He told me I could sign a last chance agreement. I knew in my heart it was time to move on, so I told him not to worry about it.

I remember walking in there on my birthday December 14, 2007, and saying to myself, "dam, I wanted to leave in a better position than this." Al pulled up in his Caddy and I walked out of Wonder bread for the last time in my life.

He stuffed some money in my pocket then he pulled the lady out and said nigga take a hit. I took a deep snort of that girl and Al said fuck that job!

He said, now you must be like me, a magician

and make magic mother fucker! Al said, remember you must believe in yourself.

These words of encouragement kept me going at the time. I knew things were going to be rough for a while.

It was good to have someone that could relate to me and give me some good advice.

When I got back to Irvington. I did not even go straight home. I had a lot on my mind. I went to a strip club for the night. When I got there. I saw this sexyass redbone Black girl. I told her to give me a Lap dance.

When I took out the money I had in my pocket, I noticed Al gave me a hundred dollars. It brought tears to my eyes that he did think enough of me to do that. When I finally got back home, my mind had a host of different things on it.

I could only sit there, lost in thoughts. After all those years and losing everything, I learned nothing last forever. Nothing!

We are just borrowers in life. Nothing is promised to us. I mean nothing. Relationships, money, family, our jobs, and everything is just for a time being. I thought at one point in my life everything would fall in place.

At the end, Sasha, and I through all the rain, there would be a sunshine of happiness. Sometimes in life, we can have all the right intentions to do the right thing. however, we must stay true to our beliefs.

That night, I sat there alone. This was my

thirty-second birthday. I had no real hope where things would go from there.

With everything stripped away from me, I knew misery and regrets would follow me for a long time. In some ways, it felt like I was trapped at times. The cold-blooded reality is nobody forced me into this life. I decided to do it.

I used to hear Al say time and time again, you must take whatever comes along with the life you choose. Time was not on my side anymore and how would I make a comeback if I could. Survival was the only thing that was on my mind.

From making tens of thousands of dollars and now reduced to making Pennies. What a turn of events. It was just like Al used to tell me, "Always be prepared to deal with everything that comes your way."

"Take advantage of whatever brakes you get and always remember nothing lasts forever."

CHAPTER 21
A WALK ON THE BOARDWALK

The year was now 2009.

Our President was the first African American president, Barack Obama, to win on a historic trip to the white house.

Our Mayor of New York city was still billionaire, Michael Bloomberg and the Richest Man in the world was still Microsoft founder, Bill Gates.

Exxon was our most powerful company. Our country's unemployment rate was at 9.5%. Since the great depression of 1929. our country was getting ready to go through a great recession.

It started in 2007, beginning with a multi-trillion dollars housing bubble burst. Big corporations would ask the government for corporate bailouts.

This would be the worst financial crisis Wall Street has ever seen. Bernie Madoff would be indicted in one of the biggest Ponzi schemes this country has ever reported in history. The poor would fall deeper into poverty.

The middle class would become poor. The richest was not the rich of yesterday anymore.

GAMBLING PROSTITUTION AND DRUGS

Now their fortunes were in jeopardy.

By this time. I was receiving unemployment, completely out of the game. The streets and the cold-blooded difficulties of life started to wear me down. It was one of the first times in my life where I felt mentally drained.

My cocaine and marijuana addiction didn't help my life and I was on a total downside. By this time, Sasha had found a place in Newark.

She pleaded with me to stay with her there for a while until she got on her feet. I had to, because it was the only right thing for me to do, considering my current situation. I would have to stay there with her in separate rooms.

I knew in my heart that eventually; Fredrick Junior would need a place to live.

Our company was still alive. I continued to pay the monthly hosting fees for the site, thinking at one point we could rebuild. However, I was hanging on to an illusion.

The reality was the two people that had this idea of building a business were no longer together. I lost my passion for this business, and I know Sasha did too.

She blamed me for the failure of Bestketsecrets but never giving me any credit for the tuff times when I held everything together. I had put up with a lot with the hopes at one point we could get back together. I did not walk out on her, although at times I wanted to.

Even to the bitter end, I stood by her. No, I

wasn't the most faithful guy in the world and the most honest at times.

This corrupted cold-blooded lifestyle we have chosen, does not breed angels! By this time, Al, and I, as close as we became, we had a falling out in the summer of 2008. He knew after I had lost everything, that the money was not coming like it was.

He knew deep down; I was in a desperate situation once again in my life. Al told me he knew someone who could give us a phony corporate loan. I mean, I was not surprised at all. He was the same person I use to walk-in real estate offices with, and Al bluntly use to say who is the crook! I want to deal with the crook!

I was never surprised at what he would say or do. The fact is, I was corrupted as he was. One night, after staying out late waiting for an associate of his who could put the scam together for us, I became undoubtedly frustrated with the situation.

When leaving early that morning, he told me I would have to meet him back in money-making Manhattan later that day, so we could meet her, and she would break down the scam.

I reluctantly agreed to meet him later that day. From that point on, that would be the last time I would speak to him until six months later.

Al had called me later that day. I didn't answer the phone.

Deep down, I was fed up with everything and

everyone. In the next six months, I collected my unemployment, and I hustled my hats and t-shirts in the car wash in Irvington.

I stayed with Sasha. We rented out a place in Newark and we stayed in separate bedrooms. At this point, I was just trying to survive the day.

Sasha and I couldn't really get back on the same page. Everything became a struggle even though she chose an alternate lifestyle. I tried to hang on as much as I could, until one day, she decided to bring Mandy up there again.

I decided after all that happened, why would you do that? She really thought, after Mandy left us like that in the critical time, we needed her.

The way she left, why would you even talk to her again. This situation infuriated me to the fullest. We had one last big argument. I decided it was time for me to go. I mean, I only stayed there because of Sasha, and I didn't want to see her struggle. However, at this point, enough is enough!

The crazy part is, I really didn't have anywhere to go. I had built up a nice little piece of a hustle in the streets with my car wash spot. I was surviving.

The reality was, I wasn't getting anywhere with Sasha. As for Bestkeptsecrets..., maybe, it was time for me to walk away. Even though I'm a fighter and hanging on to the illusion of Bestkeptsecrets' survival.

I could only tell myself that I had lost everything. Perhaps, you still have something to fight for. The reality was, for me, I didn't.

Nothing mattered anymore!

I was trapped in my own reality. Finally, my own boss.

But now, at what cost?

May of 2009, I decided after six months to contact Al and see how he was doing

It had been a while since I talked to the old gee. I went to see him in Queen's at his place. Al and I kicked it around just like old times.

It felt good to be back around him. Even for someone like Al, he also enjoyed good company. I could remember Sasha and I would still be at war with each other especially after her bringing Mandy back.

I told Al about everything I was going through. He told me I should leave; things would never be like they were. I asked Al, "could I stay with him for a while, until I figure out my next move?" After arriving at Al's, I knew the reality was I couldn't stay there with him forever—I needed my own life. I decided to go to Statesville North Carolina where my mother was living at. I decided to start over.

As much as I didn't want to leave that day, when Al was dropping me to the train station, I felt like I was leaving so much on the table. I didn't care anymore. In some ways, I was broken. I contacted my mother and I told her I was coming down there.

It didn't feel like I was being welcomed. I wasn't coming down there to stay on her and I didn't want anything from her.

I just wanted to be around family.

When Al finally dropped me to the train station. I felt a strange feeling go through my body at the time. I didn't know what that feeling was all about.

All I can say is, sometimes, you could leave a person and you don't know if that's the last time you're going to see them.

I gave Al a handshake and I said I'll see you again soon. Deep down in my heart, I didn't think I would see my old friend again.

Al said it was a pleasure having you, when I get things straight, I'm going to come to see you, Fred!

I left and got on that E train and proceeded to 34 street Pen station. North Carolina, here I come! When I got into Statesville, I had planned with my brother Robby, to come to pick me up and drop me off at a nearby motel.

I stayed a couple of nights there then I found a hotel I could rent out weekly. After a couple of weeks, I was finally getting situated in North Carolina. I stayed in a weekly rental hotel I paid for from my unemployment extension that I was riding.

I was able to survive on that for a while. I could remember Michael Jackson dying that summer. Music would never be the same again. The world had lost a legend. No matter what I did, nothing would really work out.

It wasn't for me to stay in North Carolina.

It was just for me to get away for a while. Two

months later, on August 8, on a Friday night; I would never forget this day as long as I lived. My mother, my brother and I, went to Cherokee North Carolina to Harrah's casino.

We spent the whole day there. When I got back that night in the hotel, I went right to sleep. I got up early that Saturday morning and saw that there were some missed calls from Al. I heard the phone ringing, I just let it ring out telling myself I will deal with it when I get up.

Early that Saturday morning, I tried to return Al's missed calls, no answer. This was so strange. He was the type that always answered the phone.

I remember this had happened some time back. That time, he was just sleeping off a long weekend. This time, it didn't feel like that.

It was all different. For the next two days, I tried to contact Al, still no answer. Until late Monday afternoon, my phone rang, and it was Jannette Al's girlfriend.

She told me; I hope you're sitting down? I said, "why, what's wrong?" She replies, "Al is dead, Fred!" I screamed, what!

She replied, "they found him dead in his house!" I fell to the bed in disbelief and nothing but grief; to think that they killed my friend and mentor to death.

Harlem and the streets lost a legend. The sad thing was, when he was calling, I heard the phone, I didn't pick up.

I would never know his last words or if I could

have helped or whatever the case was. A good friend of his named Andy said he spoked to Al two hours before he died.

Al said, "you see now, you have to take whatever comes along with this shit!"

With tears in my eyes, every time I think about it, every time his birthday comes, I say to myself, "I'm sorry my old friend. I didn't answer the phone."

I didn't go to the funeral because I didn't know the real reason why they killed him. And if it affected me, I didn't know because everyone knew Al and I was close.

So, I stayed away. The newspaper reported it was two guys seen leaving Al's house, getting into a nearby Lincoln.

The police contacted me, but there was nothing I could tell them. Al's murder was a mystery. The police couldn't put together a case.

Word on the street, Al was robbed. They thought the old gee, because of his flashy lifestyle was still holding on to a big stash.

However, that wasn't the truth. The cold-blooded reality was, Al got caught slipping, trusting the wrong people at the wrong time.

It catches up to all of us who think we can stay around a life of crime, which brings the most desperate and ruthless criminals.

Life is short and always not well appreciated.

Al's death made me think about my life. Was it all worth it to be shot down like that in your own residence?

The sad thing was, if I was right there with Al that night, I would be dead too. I started to question my existence and how I wanted my life to end.

September of 2009, I decided to come back to New Jersey and figure out my next move or if there is a next move. Al's death was still fresh on my mind, so I decided to give up the streets.

I mean at this point, I could really walk and cut my losses even though I would walk away broke. The reality was, I never spent more than a week in jail.

Even though I met and dealt with all kinds of individuals in the streets. I knew when to walk away and never get in too deep.

Yes, I made massive amounts of money altogether in my lifetime. In the end, I was completely broke. For whatever reasons, only the sharpest and the smartest can be marvelous.

Everything in life has a time period and after ten years, it was time for me to move on from the world of prostitution—the business that I got to know so well and learned from its ground floor. It was time for me to move on.

I was once again desperate.

This time, my desperation was to change my life. I gave up sniffing cocaine and smoking cigarettes. I started playing poker. My dream was to play in the world series of poker. I learned the game well enough to return to a place that made me miserable as a child in Atlantic City.

Poker gave me a sign of freedom. Now I could start over again. I was set free and on my own, I decided to move to Atlantic City to make my next move from there; no matter if I made it or not.

It was time for a change!

Now came the time for me to find my true self, after all these years; broke or not. I will live my life with a positive spirit, true freedom, and knowledge of self.

As I take my walk on this boardwalk, I will try to get a nice breeze from the ocean and a breath of fresh air. No more Wonder Bread, no more Bestkeptsecrets and no more pimping.

I think about all the people I met through all these life experiences. Some made me laugh and some made me cry.

Each person and each life experience I encountered will now make me strong to deal with whatever comes my way.

I'm finally free like the Seagulls you see flying around the ocean. I'm finally free!

From this point on, I will take one step at a time.

CHAPTER 22

A FLASH BACK TO THE BRICKS

It was time to start over in Atlantic city. It would eventually become my next stop. However, I wasn't finish in Newark yet; the bricks better known as Newark New Jersey. It reminded me in some ways of Brooklyn.

It was ruff and you had to hustle in this town to stay alive. Sasha and I found a way to become friends again. Fred was now living with Sasha in New York.

Her mother had sadly passed away. It was time for Sasha to move on. She stayed at her mother's house for a while with family.

It was tuff for them, losing their mother. I would always check on her place from time to time in Newark while she was at her mother's house in New York. Meanwhile, I had rented out a one bedroom in Irvington.

It was a walking distance from the car wash. Sasha found a job out there and it kept her going, to keep up with her expenses. I was still receiving unemployment and hustling my merchandise in the car wash. Sasha would eventually get laid off

GAMBLING PROSTITUTION AND DRUGS

from her job in New York and I would eventually get cut off unemployment.

Sasha copped a new girl named Cherry. Sasha brought her back to Newark. It was a strange experience at first. I had to get used to Sasha in her alternate lifestyle with her new woman.

Although, I still had feelings for her, I knew she had moved on. Cherry was a decent call girl. She was bringing Sasha a decent cash flow.

Sasha, with her experience, knew how to get a girl working right away. She had made all the contacts, escort services, brothels, all over New York city.

Only one problem with Cherry, she was an ex-drug addict. Call girls who have drug problems will always bring you short money.

Cherry stayed with Sasha about three months and then she decided to blow. They would get into an argument, and she would leave in the middle of the night. Sasha kept recruiting. She ran through several new turnouts.

However, the game was still cop and blow; money was still the motive. Meanwhile, I found a new spot across the street from the car wash.

It was a weed spot. Me and the owner became cool. He asked me if I wanted to work in there on Sundays. And I told him yes. He also agreed to let me hustle my DVDs there anytime I wanted. With this, opportunity I set up my shop right away.

It was a great opportunity for me to sell my DVDs. Both spots were generating a very lucrative cash flow until one day, the weed spot got busted! The police arrested everyone in there. The crazy thing was, they were there for weed, not my bootleg DVDs.

The cops told me, if I didn't have any warrants, I was ok. I had an old moving violation from when I was running the escort service. They had to arrest me, dam! I stayed in there about a week. Getting arrested in Newark was not like Morristown.

The prison had a twenty-three hour lock up for when you first arrived. They called it orientation. They mixed everyone together.

It didn't matter if you were a killer or there for a parking ticket like me. I was in there about a week until my sister Roxanne got me out.

My mother saved me again.

She gave Roxanne the money to get me out. They asked my father to help but he said, "let him rot in there!" It was ok. I understood his feelings towards me.

When I got back on the street, I knew I had to make some changes.

After about a week, back on the street, I ran into another hustler I had met at the car wash in Irvington. His name was Isaac.

A cool Muslim brother who had a lot of hustles about himself. When I first met Isaac, he was always impressed to see me out there early in the morning hustling. Isaac at the time was getting ready to open a store in Irvington.

He asked me if I wanted to be his partner. After

GAMBLING PROSTITUTION AND DRUGS

he told me how much rent was, I told him no. I didn't like his business practices. I noticed he wasn't sure about how he wanted to organize his business.

Time passed, and we both became cool. I would stop by his store to see him from time to time. Once, I saw Isaac, he told me he was doing very well; however, he acquired a drinking problem. He was behind on his bills and didn't know how long he can hold on. Was it an opportunity for me? I never wanted to collaborate with him.

I decided we could merge our two businesses together. Some ideas should stay an idea. I wasn't aware of how bad his drinking problem was.

He had a goldmine he put together. However, with all the drinking, he ran the business into the ground. Isaac had over leveraged himself. He was in awfully severe debt with everybody. The rent was backed up which was eighteen hundred dollars a month.

He also owed a lot of vendors some money. I came in and straighten his financial situation out. I got him back in the black within a month.

I started to see his drinking problem. He could not run a business anymore. He barely came to the store. I worked my ass off every day. I took a small cut in the stores revenue just until we could get on our feet.

One day, Isaac came in. I said to him, it is time for us to have a talk. I told him, "If he wanted me to keep working with him, it's time for him to put me on the lease." He replied, "before I do that, I rather shut the place down."

Wow!

After everything I tried to prove to you. You can't even run your business without me.

He wouldn't even put me on the lease! I said to myself, this situation will never work. I felt like I wasted my time and energy.

From that point on, I felt like, if I had stayed there any longer, I was being pimped. I did something I really didn't want to do.

Being that I oversaw the money. I took the rent. I had saved up the whole eighteen hundred dollars.

I return home later that night with the intentions to go to Atlantic City. I called Sasha and told her I was leaving in the morning. I knew Isaac would come looking for me.

This would hang over my head forever. Sometimes, we do crazy things out of anger. In his position, would he try to kill me?

Maybe, one day he will try to settle his debt. I didn't even care at the time. I ended up leaving everything in my apartment.

I said the hell with it! And I left the next morning.

CHAPTER 23
UNDER THE BOARDWALK

The next morning, I was back in Atlantic City trying to put that messy situation in Newark behind me.

I got a hotel in town and started grinding the poker tables. At first it was exciting! It felt good to get away from Newark. I played poker everywhere in Atlantic city. Some nights, I would do okay, some nights I would bust out immediately.

Poker is a tuff game.

Within a week, the sharks in Atlantic City swallowed me alive. I had lost my whole bank roll and was sitting on the boardwalk with the little luggage I had brought with me. I was now homeless with no place to go.

Dam Fred!

I checked my bags into the Tropicana casino where I had just checked out. Now it was no turning back. I just flowed around the Casinos. I started to meet a lot of different people who was in the same situation as me or even worse. Being homeless was tuff at first. It's not a situation that just grows on you.

When those lights go out at night on the street and that cold air hits you then the raw reality sets in, you have no place to go.

I have never been in a situation like this before. I had mixed feelings of feeling like a true looser or unlucky. This strange scenario would give me a sense of true freedom. At this point, I had nothing more to lose.

I knew this from looking at other people who I had seen homeless on the street. The one thing they avoided was keeping their self-clean. I found places, bathrooms, and spots all over Atlantic City I could go.

I had a good spot to take a quick shower across the street from the Golden Nugget. It was where the boats would come and there was no lock on the bathrooms. If you were smooth about it, you could dip in and out.

When I didn't have a choice, I would go right there.

Casinos are always a place you can meet people. A good casino hustler thrives off the casino life like a whore takes to a trick.

These people are addicted to the action in the attraction of the life. From the pimps to the whores, and to the gamblers, somebody is always being hustled. It's the nature of the casino environment.

Until I started meeting high rollers that could take me into the high roller lounges, I ate at the local soup kitchens around Atlantic city. I slept in the casino bus lobbies. My favorite casino was the Show Boat casino.

The casino security would let us sleep in the bus lobby some nights then in the morning, security would come and kick all of us out. I would go to Bally's casino horse in poker room and that's where I would hustle during the day.

I would follow all casino promotions where you could scrape up extra money to stay in action. Staying in action is the blood line to any gambler. A true gambler will do anything to make his or her last bet.

Casinos will never tell you they thrive off the casino hustler. By that time, my mother would come up with her husband or by herself, she used to let me stay in her room. My mother at that time was a high roller in most of the casinos she went in.

She was a legendary casino hustler that made a living in Atlantic city for years.

Everybody knew her in the town.

She taught me the ins and outs of the casino business.

I had some great times with her that would stay with me forever. When she was there, I wanted for nothing. When she left, I went back to my normal routine.

I was very determined to survive this situation I was going through. I played poker as much as I could.

However, I knew the key to being a successful

gambler is to keep a bankroll. A professional gambler number one's best asset is developing or having self-discipline.

Some gamblers are born with it, some develop it in time. However, without this attribute you will find yourself broke most of the time.

Remember, gambling is more of a mental psychology than anything. I couldn't afford to go broke. I had no one to count on.

I ran into a guy named Mike. He was an old-school ex Italian book maker from Boston. He beat me in a hand at a cash game in Bally's poker room.

He was one of the best in Atlantic city. He was a legendary poker player who had already been on Tv. Mike broke the game down to me like a science.

He didn't like a lot of people around him. I guess, we were alike in some ways. He was a high roller. In Total Rewards casinos, he took me to all the lounges with him. Mike had a fetish for real slutty hookers.

He would risk his last dollars playing craps. Mike had a genuine real old school mafia type of swag about him. He used to say, "Fred, as long as you pay the tax, you can stay with me in my rooms."

This situation had worked out well until a hooker he was messing with got mad at me. She told Mike I was trying to take advantage of him. Mike and I parted ways. It was ok. I really didn't want to depend on anyone.

It had been some time and I haven't gone to

Newark. It was the first time in my life other than when I was a kid. I spent so much time in Atlantic City. I had already been there six months. My birthday and the holidays were in a month.

Atlantic City is surrounded by water. It is a beautiful summer resort. It always has been. The winters are brutal. It's the slowest time of the year for Atlantic City.

I needed to find ways to keep surviving. I wasn't going back to Newark until I had a plan. I had already planted that reality in my head.

I would call from time to time to check up on Sasha and Fred and if I had extra money, I would send it. I knew in my heart this would be the only way I can find myself.

This reality was setting in.

All my hustling days, I would never forget this day. I had hustled up some money from playing horses. The Golden Nugget casino was running a poker promotion—five hundred dollars for the high hand every hour.

I sat down at a random table I bought in for sixty dollars. And after about ten minutes of sitting there the dealer deals me an ace deuce of diamonds suited.

The flop gave me a diamond draw with a deuce. The other player was on a bigger draw. He pushed me all in.

The turn card gave him another deuce which gave him a full house. WOW! One more card to go... the river gave me the fourth deuce.

I had quads, yes! I took a deep breath with excitement. I won the high hand and the money in the pot... call it what you want. I called it hustler's luck.

From that point on, everything started to change for me. The Golden Nugget became my new spot.

The Golden Nugget was running a promotion for high tier casino cards which I was able to get one. I was a regular in the Nugget high rollers lounge.

I also knew other people that would take me. The casino started giving me complimentary rooms; two to three nights a week.

Some days, I didn't have to sleep in the casino bus lobby. I could take showers like a normal person, and I didn't gamble a lot from day to day.

I just lived the casino life.

I was now a casino hustler, and this would be the only way I could survive right now.

CHAPTER 24
THE CASINO BUS CIRCUIT

While sitting in the bus lobby, I notice a lot of fellow gamblers coming in and going out of town.

Casino buses was the way all these casinos stayed alive through the tristate area. It was casino mania. I remember a fellow gambler giving me the rundown on where to catch the casino bus and what casinos promotions was the best.

At this point, the Chinese controlled the casino bus industry. I mean... literally, they controlled it. You could close your eyes and just pick a casino.

It was a great time to be a gambler and the bus was a great option, especially if you were on the street. I met a guy named David Jones, who was an ex-wall street hustler.

David had a great head for numbers and was a naturally smart individual. I met him through another casino hustler named Mark.

I would never forget some conversations I had with David. He once told me if they could put a man on the moon then craps can be beaten.

He gave me the run down about Foxwoods. David had come to Atlantic city with the inspirations to play poker. He had fell in love with craps. In later years, he would scam the casinos out of hundreds of thousands of dollars.

He was one of the top casino hustlers in the game who lost his whole life to gambling. He put me on to some money moves that helped me in the casino business. At that time, you could close your eyes and pick a casino.

Let's say, you had Sands which use to be on Atlantic cities boardwalk. It was now located in Bethlehem Pennsylvania.

It is now called Wind Creek. This bus ride was the hardest to get on all the Chinese immigrants, and high roller Chinese baccarat players rode this bus, with the bus having such horrible conditions to travel on.

It was a day-to-day hustle for the Chinese and anyone else that could ride. The casino bus circuit was a different world within itself. You had to ride to earn.

These people rode the bus every day, so it was impossible to get on the Sands bus. The Sands bus package would cost you fifteen dollars for the bus ticket and a mandatory five-dollar tip to the Chinese host who sold you the ticket which they would split with the driver of the bus.

When you arrived at the casino, you will receive a forty-five-dollar slot play. The Chinese had it set where they would buy your slot play off you for thirty-eight dollars. Everybody made their piece of the pie.

The Chinese controlled the whole underground casino industry in every casino.

The Sands had the best casino bus package, so this bus was heavily in demand.

David one day took me to Foxwoods casino in Connecticut to show me the whole run down and where to get the buses from in Flushing, New York, the new China town.

I was right back at home. The casino buses weren't too far from the old shea stadium. Now renamed Citi Field, it was perfect; I knew the area.

I felt comfortable in Queens. I didn't like Foxwoods or at least, I didn't understand his science behind it. He also showed me the two casinos in New York city: Empire casino located in the Bronx and the world Resorts was in Queens where Aqueduct Racetrack was located.

World Resorts was the top grossing casino in the country. Mohegan sun, not too far from Foxwoods was giving out a hundred-dollar slot play if you had any ALANTIC City casino card.

This was my opportunity to make some money. I knew a casino hustler named Arc. He showed me where in China town in New York city to get the bus. He was like my personal tour guide for Mohegan sun.

And of course, he asked me for a couple of dollars after I got the slot play. Mohegan sun started to become one of my favorite runs in time to come.

It was time for me to join the bus circuit. After

the trip to Mohegan sun with Arc, I decided it was time to leave Atlantic City for a while.

I wasn't going to return to Newark without any progress. I found a seat on the Sands bus at night, then a fellow bus rider helped me get a seat on the Sands bus in the daytime.

Both buses left from Flushing.

The situation in the new hustle worked out to my advantage.

From all my hustling experience, I was going to find a way to make it work. My first month riding the bus, I didn't sell my package like everyone else did.

I would play mines on a machine called quick hits and would at least make my money from the bus or sometime a profit. I had great luck with the machine! By that time, I had got even better at poker. I would take my money and go play poker as well.

Sands had a great poker room, and no one knew me. Now, I became the shark grinding. ALANTIC CITY poker rooms prepared me for war when I visited the rest of these poker rooms around the tri state area.

This was truly an adventure for me. I loved it in the beginning. It didn't matter that I was truly homeless with nowhere to go. I LOVED MY FREEDOM. Though I wasn't successful, however, the everyday worries of this world I escaped. There were some days I missed my old life.

In some way or another, I felt like this was a

new beginning for me. I didn't know exactly where this road would lead me. At this point in my life, I was tuff mentally because the last eight months had made me so.

Being homeless in Atlantic City showed me strengths I never knew I had. I had to learn how to adjust. I started going to Newark to see Sasha and Fred before I would go back on my daily bus runs.

It felt good to see them after eight months in Atlantic City. They were surviving. Sasha was renting out some rooms in her apartment and Fred was going to school. I told them I was going to leave in the morning and told them about my new venture.

At least, I was doing ok. I left the next morning with happiness just to see my family again. I gave them some money and told her to call me if she has any problems.

I was on my next adventure!

CHAPTER 25

FROM A SHOESTRING

The Sands run helped me organize myself. With my cash flow, I decided if I'm going to be on the streets, it made sense for me to find a place to keep my clothes and the rest of my belongings.

Flushing was a dream area for people who was on the streets. The first move I made was I got a small storage unit from Cube Smart.

The second move I made was I got a gym membership at the city parks facility for fifty dollars for every six months. Now, I can take showers regularly.

At nights, I slept on the bus. The third move I made; I got a post office box. Now, I can receive mail. The fourth move I made was I open a checking account.

The object was to hustle the bus circuit and do this with taking limited risk. I watched the Chinese.

They are great hustlers, and I was extremely impressed. I was fully organized at this point. I had money moves for every casino in the bus circuit. Empire casino became my strong hold in New York city with the card hustle David had showed me.

It was no telling what I could make on the jacks and better one dollar poker machine which I had learned how to play in Atlantic City.

The card hustle worked well every day at Empire casino. They would give a certain amount of slot play on every player's card. It just required for the player to put on a certain number of points on the card to receive it.

Five days a week, Empire casino had a promotion. I had bought cards from everybody. I started with my family members like my son and my sister.

Then I bought cards from certain people on the bus who wasn't using their card. I had up to fifteen cards at one time. The number of cards I had was okay with me. It was enough for me to create an income stream with.

The Chinese was greedy. Some would get caught with a hundred cards at one time. I guess the way they looked at it is, the most they can do was throw us out the casino.

I had to hustle Empire casino over the next two years. Until one day riding the bus, I said to myself while riding, what's next for me after this?

Then I decided, why not write a book? I had hit a lonely point in my life. I wanted to put all my life experiences on paper.

Maybe I can find some people who can identify with my story. When I first started writing, it was tuff. However, I was determined to try to at least write one book in my lifetime.

I would read and write every day when I got off the bus from whatever casino I was leaving from. It was usually Foxwoods. Foxwoods was a cool ride at night.

I rode the second to the last bus leaving for Foxwood every night. It was a three-hour ride to Foxwoods. It was plenty of time from going and coming to finally get some sleep. By the time the bus got up there, it was a 2am bus leaving back to Flushing.

I would sell my package, jump on that bus and ride back to Flushing. By the time the bus got back to Flushing, it was 5am in the morning and a local Starbucks was open.

I would sit in there every day, reading and writing until writing became a part of my life.

I would leave from Starbucks every day, go to my storage and then the gym to take a shower. This became part of my daily routine.

I was surviving now. Not only was I surviving, but I also had a plan of action. There was something pushing me to do better.

I had decided at one point I was going to start my own publishing company. Even if I had just written one book, I said to myself, I would walk around the streets and sell it. At one point, I wanted to stop riding the bus. It was like I was moving in quicksand.

I wanted to do more in life than just gamble or hustle for money. I wanted to share my story with other people. It didn't matter the dollar amount of which I made. I just wanted my life to have meaning.

Writing gave me that therapy I needed to escape from the world, even if it was for a couple of moments. I had got a bigger unit at Cube Smart. My bill was now a hundred and forty dollars a month. I turned it into a small office.

With everything in a five-to-ten-mile radius, it was very easy to get around without having a vehicle. One of the reasons I wrote this book; I wanted it to be a true testimonial for other people that, it doesn't matter what we have been through in life, we can all change and make greater impacts for ourselves.

We can take our negatives and turn them into positives if we find the desire in our heart. No matter how hard it is at this point, I knew in my heart I had to change.

I felt this intrinsic motivation all over me.

I became humble at one point in my life. Money, cars, success, etc. really didn't matter anymore. All that mattered was eating or just sleeping that day.

The days when I stood in lines at those soup kitchens, if you had told me ten years ago that would be me, I would have said back then, that would never happen to me.

Today, if you talk to me, I will tell you I have met people from all walks of life that was homeless. So, this could happen to anyone.

With this greedy capitalistic society, we live in,

it will happen to even more.

Never think it could never be you. I had to learn how to adjust being homeless in just appreciate the simple things in life. It took me a long time to accept being humble.

From a shoestring, just like when I was a kid, I saw my Pops start his business. On the other hand, he gave me a lifetime of courage.

From a shoestring, just like Sasha and I started our company, I learned the pro and cons of starting and running a company.

From a shoestring, it's very good to start small as long as you get started. Greed, ambition, and dreamers, which one are you?

They say these are the true ingredients to the entrepreneurial recipe to success.

With my experience in wisdom, these feelings are in all of us. The only thing to fear is fear itself.

The biggest elements to success are how do I get started? What are your motivating factors?

What holds us back could eventually kill us.

The sad part is, we are all sitting on natural wealth and some of us just don't know it.

You therefore need to wake up and come to this realization. You need to find self, just like I did.

If only you can "discover self," "do what's required" and "sweat the sweats," then you can "bag the achievements."

Finally,

I am hopeful that if you can only get one thing out of this book, that you should be fighting for your dreams no matter what.

The days of being a faithful employee are long gone.

We must find our calling in life and go for it. Find that motivating factor in your life and hunt for that "true financial freedom."

It's all out there waiting for all of us. What business will you start from a shoestring? What gets you up in the morning?

Let's not focus on just becoming rich overnight. This could result to a disaster and ruin our lives forever.

We must develop a strategic mindset for success and sometimes, it can be a very slow process.

A good plan over time works in life. Sometimes, we always must change our strategy. I learned in life that gambling it's not a sprint.

Becoming financially free is a marathon run. It's not about winning; its more about just staying consistent through the whole race and remaining focused.

In the end, reading my story and connecting with my ordeals has shown it's not about a big success story of a guy who made millions of dollars, or who had mansions and rode assorted cars.

I'm just a guy who grew up in South Queens.

An ordinary guy who found essence in telling his story.

I'm sure it wasn't the greatest book nor the

worst book.

However, everyone has a story to tell; good or bad.

I only hope, whoever reads this book can learn from my life experiences.

THANK YOU FOR READING **GAMBLING PROSTITUTION AND DRUG**
IN MEMORY OF RIP TO William and Rosa lee Jackson. Rip to Jeffrey Jackson Rip TO Mike and Billy Jackson Rip to Edna Seymour Rip to Colen N Toomer RIP Alan Robinson and Alan Jr Robinson. Rip to Darren Rogers.

ABOUT THE AUTHOR

Hello readers. My name is Frederick Lee Toomer, the author of this book. This book is written, based on a true story about my life.

Names of some characters in this book have been changed to protect their identities.

This book tells the story of my life, the times, and crimes of the corrupted NEW YORK City Streets.

The purpose and content in this book are to take you through my childhood life experiences, into a world of **GAMBLING PROSTITUTION AND DRUGS**.

I will share all these experiences with you and give you the horrific end to a life of crime. Please, enjoy my story about GAMBLING PROSTITUTION AND DRUGS, as presented by F. READYPUBLISHING.

Made in the USA
Columbia, SC
06 October 2022